The Armour of God

Steve Higgs

To all the women who choose to enter male dominated environments and refuse to be intimidated by the ratio against them. I have met very few who ticked both boxes, but those who did proved there was no reason why they shouldn't be there.

Here's to them.

Contents

Chapter 1

November 2013,
Rochester, England

The portal opened on to the dark cobbles at the side of the cathedral in Rochester. We were home again, and as my feet touched the familiar street, it made the last few days seem like a dream. That was until I looked at my hands.

In my right was a sword. The so-called sword of God, an ancient artefact forged by demons many thousands of years before. It was black like obsidian, razor sharp and I could channel source energy through it. In my left hand, which is prosthetic, I held the hand of a demon. His name is Daniel and I had him to thank for my escape from hell. He had willingly stepped up to free me from the binding another demon called Nathaniel had over me and in so doing has surely sealed his own doom.

Nathaniel was dead, killed by me when I plunged the God sword through his heart and pushed hellfire into it. He was the first demon to die in over four thousand years, since their supreme leader was betrayed and murdered by one of his sons and released a death curse with his dying breath.

The curse tore the demons from the Earth, ditching them into a parallel realm where they became immortal, doomed to live forever trapped in a plane from which there was no escape. They couldn't reproduce, they wouldn't age, but the death curse was losing its potency. Like ripples on a pond, they were dying down and the demons, and other magical creatures, were beginning to find their way through to the mortal realm of men again.

They planned to return, believing the death curse would soon fail completely, and when that happened, they would subjugate mankind and rule the Earth as before. They were imbued with magic, able to manipulate elements, control creatures, and wield power of intense magnitude. I was yet to learn the full range of what they might be capable of doing and this gap in my knowledge came about because I had no idea they even existed until a few days ago.

Since arriving in the ancient English city of Rochester a little more than a week ago, I had discovered supernatural creatures, been kidnapped, found myself enslaved more than once and now I possessed what might very well be the most powerful weapon on Earth.

I released Daniel's hand, swapping the sword from my right to left because I needed to scratch my face and preferred to do it with my real hand.

'They will come after us,' Daniel murmured, articulating my thoughts, but I had no idea they would find us so soon, for the moment the words left his mouth, the air began to shimmer just a few yards away.

Daniel grabbed my hand, tugging me along as he began to run, but as we tried to put some distance between ourselves and the portal about to open, the same shimmering circles of air, like ripples on a vertical pond, began to form in every other direction we could choose to look.

'How did they find us so quickly?' I gasped in frustration.

'They were close to us,' Daniel growled, as he readied himself to fight. 'They must have seen the cathedral in the background, and someone recognised it.' I knew from experience that when the portal opens, there is a very brief moment when one can see what is on the other side. It's a bit like opening one door and stepping into a very small room before opening the door on the other side, but the doors are both open for just that split second.

I swore and yanked my hand free of Daniel's as we both drew in source energy to form weapons. The familiar tickle of source energy crackled under my skin, sparks arcing over the surface of my right shoulder and down to my hand where it formed a glowing blue orb. This was sinfire, the form my body chose to create with source energy. It was less potent than hellfire, which I haven't yet worked out how to produce, but just as deadly depending on how I employed it.

With his back against mine, Daniel's own palms were filled with red orbs. Something all demons had taught themselves to create, hellfire would kill anything living if it touched them. Anything but me, it seemed. I was able to absorb it, spindling the energy inside myself where it charged me like a battery, waiting to be discharged.

There was nowhere to run as perhaps two dozen portals coalesced in the grounds in front of the cathedral. The area had been subject to several battles in the last few days with me at the centre of two of them. I guess that was why there wasn't a person in sight tonight when the tourist attraction would normally be teeming with life.

Through gritted teeth, I growled, 'Here they come,' as the first portal opened. Shilt, lizard-like magical creatures able to conjure a veil that made them appear human, poured through the portal and directly into a stream of deadly sinfire energy that killed them as fast as they could enter the mortal realm. Holding a stream of energy was another mystical gift I appeared to have which very few others possessed. It enabled me to power the God sword, but that was for close quarter fighting and I didn't want these things anywhere near me.

More portals opened and more shilt came, but then I spotted ogres too. Giant lumbering bipedal beasts, they worked with the shilt, controlling them to greatly enhance their effectiveness.

'We have demons!' shouted Daniel. He was behind me, firing as fast as he could, but this was a concentrated attack and there was no hope of fighting them all.

'Are they attacking?' I yelled over my shoulder, throwing more sinfire into yet another portal and killing another dozen shilt. It was already beginning to feel like we were trying to hold back the sea, and yet more of the portals were opening.

I heard a grunt from Daniel before he answered. 'Not yet. It's Gershwin, Rebecca, and Lester. They all have a grudge against me and will be wanting to further their own ambitions by bringing me back to Beelzebub.'

The ruler of the demons wanted the sword. That came as no surprise, nor did his reluctance to come after it himself. I had just killed one of his generals using it so he would deploy foot soldiers like the shilt and tempt lesser demons to come after it first. If they succeeded, he would reward them. If I killed them, he hadn't lost much.

An ogre was organising a body of shilt – I just couldn't kill them all fast enough – and he had an energy shield which they all hid behind. My sinfire hit it but discharged outwards harmlessly into the air and ground.

They were going to overwhelm us if we stayed in one place.

'We should go!' Daniel shouted over the noise of battle. 'There's too many! Take my hand!'

The ogre now had something in his hand and was beginning to twirl it. Was it a set of bolas? That's what it looked like, but the answer was less important than knowing what damage it might do. Daniel wanted to flee. To open a portal and evade them by keeping in motion. But where would that end? If we escaped being overwhelmed here by shifting to another place in the mortal or immortal realms, then they would follow. They might not know where we had gone, but they would find us eventually.

I didn't want to keep running. I wanted to scare the crap out of them now and make them think twice about coming after me.

Daniel reached his hand out to take mine, but I yanked it away from his grasp. 'No. I have a better plan.' Daniel loosed two red orbs into a pack of shilt and swivelled around to face me. 'I'm going to kill a few demons,' I snarled. 'Keep them off my back.'

I didn't give him time to argue; it wasn't a discussion. If he wanted to run, he could go, but I was making a stand here and I wanted the demons to shoot at me.

The ogre had to be dealt with first though. Its right arm was above its head, the bolas a blur of red light now. He was going to launch them in the space of the next heartbeat, but to do so he was going to have to shift his shield. I didn't have to wait, which was a good thing because there were shilt pressing in from every side and the demons, more than three now, were throwing hellfire our way.

Daniel caught it or deflected it, but not every shot. Some made it through, pummelling him even as he tried to fight back. He staggered a pace, and I left him to manage on his own as I ran at the ogre. Its shield twitched a little to the left and in the split second between it moving and his throw, I sent him a sustained burst of sinfire.

It wouldn't kill him, not the way it did the shilt, but it slammed into him, shunting him backwards and ruining his aim. The bolas went wild, ripping across the open space in front of the cathedral until they met another demon stepping through a freshly opened portal.

I felt, rather than saw, the explosion because I was still running at the ogre. It wasn't the only ogre on the field of battle, but it was the biggest and had the most shilt around it. I was going to see just what damage I could do up close.

Shutting off my stream of sinfire, I switched the sword back into my right hand. My left was now all but useless to fight with; I couldn't channel sinfire into it, and that was something I needed to consider for future encounters, but drawing in yet more source energy, I pushed arcing blue magic into the sword and got to watch the faces around me light up in fear as the glossy black blade began to glow from the inside.

My blast of sinfire had thrown the ogre backward into the shilt gathered behind him, toppling many of them like bowling pins. His shield faltered as he fell, but he would be back on his feet before I reached him, and I couldn't produce more sinfire without switching sword hands again. Seeing this, the nearest of the shilt foolishly attacked me.

The shilt are hive creatures. Asexual by nature, they have no gender but reproduce in great numbers. They feed on life energy, sucking it from their victims to leave lifeless husks behind. They had tried that on me the night I discovered my powers, one could even blame them for my becoming, but whatever it is that is special about me, when I kill a shilt, it simply disintegrates.

My pace didn't slow as I swept the sword upward through the first creature. Nor when I decapitated the second. Others were too close to get out of my way and they fell too, their bodies turning to dust or ash as I ran through them with the blade.

The ogre was back on its feet and able to bring its shield back to life just before I got to it. The translucent rectangle of energy was two yards across and almost three high, which it needed to be in order for the ogre to hide behind it. The creature thrust its shield forward to fend me off and looked surprised when I drove the point directly through the shield and into its chest.

With a scream, I poured sinfire through the sword, exploding the ogre from the inside.

Think I'm a bit bloodthirsty? Think I am murderous? None of this was my idea. I moved to Rochester to take up a research job in a library. I used to be a soldier, and still might be if I hadn't been too close to my sergeant when he stepped on a landmine. I lost my left hand and left foot and had a piece of shrapnel tear through the left side of my face. The tiny sliver of metal ripped into my brain where it remains to this day. It destroyed much of my memory and could shift position at any point, killing me in an instant. The funny part of that was the doctors' advice to avoid fast or jerky movements, and above all, avoid hitting my head.

The sword came free again as the ogre came apart and I spun on the spot, sweeping the blade around in a wide circle at neck height where two shilt were about to skewer me with their own short swords.

Killing the ogre made everyone pay attention, but it didn't stop them from attacking. The shilt were swarming Daniel who appeared to have been beaten back by hellfire blasts from the demons. I suspected Beelzebub wanted to make an example of him, and his instruction most likely was to capture him at all costs. From what I knew of him,

Daniel had risen steadily through the demon caste system to become a major player. He'd achieved that by finding humans to enslave - I never said he was a good guy. I needed him though, to move between realms, and to fill in some of the many blanks I had. So, it was time to rescue him; if he got taken back to hell, he was as good as lost to me. Beelzebub might not be able to kill him, but he could inflict a lot of pain and put him somewhere I wouldn't be able to retrieve him from.

Switching the sword into my left hand yet again, I fired pulses of light blue sinfire into the mass of bodies surrounding him. The shilt had been able to get close enough to use their strength to nullify his weapons. Unable to form hellfire orbs, because they had his hands pinned, Daniel would have to resort to elemental magic to defend himself, and as I thought that, I could feel the hair on my head begin to rise as he pulled static electricity inward. He was agitating the air, something I'd seen others do, though mostly mortal wizards, not demons or angels who considered the use of elemental magic almost beneath them.

I had been about to charge in to free him but changed direction fast when I sensed he was about to pull lightning down onto himself. He did so in the next second, but I didn't get to see it. Focussed on Daniel, I had taken my eyes off the demons. There were maybe a dozen of them now – I wasn't going to stand still and get an exact count – and they were all on the periphery of the fight, standing back to let the shilt do the dirty work. Together they blasted Daniel into submission, concentrating their hellfire until he collapsed and the shilt could overpower him. With him down, their aim shifted.

Onto me.

I didn't see it coming, and so had no warning nor opportunity to do anything to defend myself. Half a dozen ... heck, maybe it was ten or more, bolts of hellfire struck my body. The wall of energy picked me up like a candy wrapper in the wind, tossing me across the grass backside over teakettle. Mercifully, I wasn't on the cobbles at the time or the blow to my head as it slammed into the ground might have knocked me out. As it was, I saw stars and tasted blood and could hear nothing but a high-pitched whine for a moment.

The demons were daft enough to gloat about beating me to the ground and bright enough to continuing firing their hellfire orbs into me now that I was down. Like I said earlier, hellfire kills mortals, all except me, who, for some reason as yet unexplained, can spindle it in my body. I don't know how much I can take, but quite a bit it seems because as their blasts continued to pummel my body, I started to get up.

In a crouch, with the sword in my left hand and my prosthetic knuckles pushing me off the dirt, I got to show the demons my teeth as I regained my feet. I had to lean forward to stay upright, but seeing their best shots were having little to no effect on me, the demons efforts dwindled and then stopped.

I had a clear circle around me now, the shilt running for cover to get away from the hellfire and that gave me a few seconds of time. I felt full to the brim with hellfire energy, but not like when you eat a huge meal and make a pig of yourself to then feel uncomfortable; this felt like some kind of magical upgrade, like I'd just been fitted out with a turbo thruster.

My meagre chest heaved as I sucked in a lungful of air and raised my right hand. Instead of light blue, this time the stream of energy that flew from my open palm was dark red, almost black, in fact, but with light blue sparkles woven through it like glitter.

I swung it in the direction of Daniel, turning a squadron of shilt to ash in a heartbeat. The demon was on the ground, and he had a dozen of the shilt short swords sticking from his body. He would recover quickly enough but this hadn't been a fun experience for him, and he would need some new clothes.

Now that he was free, I started running again. There were still shilt here; together we had succeeded in killing only half of the force so far, but I didn't care about them any longer. Yes, in theory they could hurt me, so too the ogres, of which I could see three, but I wanted the demons.

They had drifted into a gaggle when they pummelled Daniel and then me, and that made them a fun target. They got the same blast of hellfire I gave the shilt, but here's another thing about me: the stream I can create pushes constant source energy out. It won't kill the demons because they are immortal, but it will put them down.

I couldn't get them all, but as I ran at them, leaving Daniel to pick himself up, I gave it my best shot. Some tried to fire back, which was laughable given that their hellfire had fuelled me in the first place. It was like being reloaded as I fired. I spotted two escaping, a portal of shimmering air appearing for them to dive through, but they would not all have time.

I had to cross a portion of the stone plaza in front of the cathedral, the change to a solid surface allowing me to accelerate since my feet no longer slipped on the wet dirt and grass, and then I was upon them.

I dropped the stream of energy just long enough to get the sword back into my right hand and then lit it up as before. The first downward slash took a demon's head off. I didn't know her name and doubted I ever would. The surprise on her face would stick with me though. Blood flew in an arc, coating her beautiful dress and splashing onto me as I charged through her headless body. By the time it hit the ground her body was already turning to dust and I was killing the next demon, this time a male.

I got three of them before the rest scattered and formed portals, and a fourth before he was able to step through to safety.

To my left, Daniel was shooting again, proving how quickly demons can recover from terrible injuries. However, when I turned to see what might be left for me to do, the last of the shilt vanished through a portal and the area was suddenly silent.

Except for the wailing sirens that is.

Chapter 2

Daniel and I were both breathing heavily, the effort and adrenalin raising our pulse rates. His would calm a lot faster than mine, but out of breath or not, we needed to be somewhere else.

'Do you think they will try that again?' I asked, slowly spinning on the spot to make sure there wasn't a fresh batch of portals beginning to open.

'How many demons did you kill?' he asked.

'Four.'

He shook his head and blew a hard breath out through his nose. 'I think you just bought us some grace. The demons will have to get used to the concept that they can be killed, and it is going to scare the pants off them. I don't think they will be back tonight.'

'They will be back though,' I stated. 'We will have to be ready.'

Daniel gave me a grim look. 'Beelzebub will send his best next time. He wants that sword.'

'I think Godfrey does too,' I commented, naming the leader of the angels and Beelzebub's brother.

Daniel nodded. 'Given what it can do, anyone who can wield it will want it.'

The sirens were coming closer and we were standing in a war zone. The cathedral looked to have been attacked with a wrecking ball. Windows were smashed and brickwork lay on the ground all around us. Several of the large stone squares that make the floor of the plaza were broken and jutting up at odd angles where stray hellfire energy had struck.

I started moving, getting around to the front of the cathedral where I was reminded of the previous battle. Hoarding was still in place by Northgate, the ancient entrance to the city. It was there to keep people back and explained why there was no one around tonight – the area was shut off. There would be similar barriers at the other entrances, I felt sure.

Fortunately, I knew a way out of here that didn't involve any of the entrances. On the High Street side of the cathedral, a small parade of shops selling cream teas, confectionary and such like, hides an alleyway that runs around the back. At the end of that, I had Daniel boost me up so I could clamber over a wall. At a pinch over five feet tall, a wall doesn't have to be very high to defeat me and it doesn't help that my left hand isn't real.

Dropping down the other side, I waited two seconds for Daniel to join me, hid the sword inside his jacket, and paused to arrange my hoody. The left side of my face, from just about the centre of my cheek, all the way up to above level with my left eye, is a patchwork of scar tissue. The shrapnel did a real job on me and not yet six months on, I am still very self-conscious about it. I don't like being stared at. Can you blame me? Content that I was hidden, I looped my arm through Daniel's, and we sauntered out onto the High Street pretending to be a couple out for the evening.

The High Street wasn't what I expected though. Usually, Rochester's ancient architecture and myriad bars, restaurants, and taverns attracts a big crowd. Recent events must have put most people off because it was almost deserted.

I say almost deserted because there were a few people inside the bars and restaurants I could see into, and there was a gathering of people by Northgate to our left. They had undoubtedly been drawn there by the lights and noise of our battle and they were even now trying to peer around the edge of the temporary barrier. The barrier was there because a wizard called Otto Schneider had buried an ogre and a dozen shilt in a hole the other side of the gate just a few days ago. I was there when that happened and still there when a secret agency showed up to take over the scene from the police. They seemed somehow to know about the demons and supernatural and they probably wanted to speak to me, but I managed to slip away when they were kicking the police out.

Talking of the police, the sirens we had been listening to jumped in volume as two squad cars appeared at the bridge end of the High Street. It was time to go. Steering Daniel around to face the other way,

I wasn't entirely sure where I was going to go now that I was back in the mortal realm and had just one idea in my head.

It went sideways instantly when I faced away from the cops and found I was being stared at by a man blocking our way.

'Anton?' I gasped. Then to Daniel, I whispered, 'Be cool. He's a friend.'

I didn't exactly know Anton; he was a barman in Eddy's Tavern, the pub that sits at the bridge end of Rochester High Street. He was kind to me and helpful when I first arrived in the city. I was all alone and wanted to keep to myself, mostly because of my terrible facial scars from the shrapnel, but he didn't seem to care about them. Not that this was a sexual thing, he was just being nice, and in return, I led Nathaniel and his gang of thug demons to the bar and left it virtually destroyed.

'I thought that was you,' he replied. He still had on his barman's clothes; the sleeves of his shirt rolled up to reveal the tattoos on his forearms.

'Did the bar survive?' I asked, pulling a face because when I last saw it, there were flames licking out of the windows.

He tilted his head slightly and shrugged. 'It hardly matters, but the damage is mostly superficial.' He wasn't saying things that he wanted to say, biting his top lip and looking me up and down.

I knew what it was he wasn't saying. 'You saw me, didn't you?'

He nodded his head slowly. 'You asked me about heaven and hell and the supernatural. I guess I have an idea why now. Those people you were fighting, what are they?'

'Demons,' I replied quietly. Behind us one of the police cars blipped its siren once to get people to move out of their way. I twitched but didn't turn around to look. Meeting Anton's eyes, I said, 'I really need to be somewhere else. There is trouble coming.'

He nodded again, twitching his eyes to look at Daniel for the first time and then back at me. 'Are you a demon too?' Anton asked.

I opened my mouth to say no, but then stopped myself because I don't know what I am. 'I'm not sure,' I admitted. 'I really do have to go though.' However, just as I was about to push past him, I stopped myself. I had no right to ask anything of him, but I was going to anyway. 'Anton, can I please use your phone? I need to call Alex.' He knew my friend; she was a regular in his pub.

His eyes flared in surprise, but he said, 'Sure,' and dug it from a back pocket. My own phone was long gone, lost to the police when they arrested me ... was that yesterday? I thought maybe it was the day before. All I knew was I hadn't slept in what felt like forever, I was likewise starved, my phone, bank cards, and everything else I needed to operate as a human being in the twenty first century were gone and the hordes of hell were coming for me as well as the police because I was still wanted for murdering my flatmate and then busting out of jail.

Neither of which I was guilty of, I should add.

There were things I had to do: eat and sleep were on the list, but they were not at the top because staying alive felt more pressing. I wanted to call Alex. I didn't have many friends; there hadn't been time to make them yet since I'd only been here a few days and most of them were spent fighting for my life. Alex worked at the library, we were similar in age, and she'd come to my rescue when a wizard attacked me. She got hurt in the exchange, although not badly, but had then pitched in to help me because she saw me form and fire sinfire with my right hand. Together with another girl, Abigail, who also worked at the library, they were already (sort of) aware of the supernatural world. To my surprise, there was an underground web of theorists tracking events around the globe and they, in turn, were suspicious that a clandestine organisation was trying to shut them down.

It was that organisation who showed up to push the police out of the cathedral grounds and they were allegedly called the Supernatural Investigation Alliance though their vans had been marked as Special Investigations Bureau. I needed Alex for several reasons, not least of which was she could provide me with somewhere to crash for the night.

I couldn't remember her number though.

'You okay?' asked Anton when he saw me grimace at his phone.

I handed it back. 'I thought I might remember her number, but I guess no one does that anymore.'

Next to me and still with my arm looped through his, Daniel was becoming agitated. It was a new look for him. Until a few hours ago, he had been the most calm and completely together person I had ever met. The difference was all to do with his power mountain collapsing. He'd been edging into Beelzebub's inner circle, but now he was demon public enemy number one and they would do awful things if they captured him.

'It's not far to her house from here,' I commented as I started to walk. 'Thank you, Anton. I'm really sorry about the Tavern.'

Before I could leave him behind, Anton said something that truly surprised me. He asked, 'Can I help you?'

'Help me?' I echoed.

He shrugged and started to walk backwards in the direction I had been heading. 'You were about to go this way, right? I've seen things on television tonight. It was the same thing I saw here in the High Street. What happened here was happening all over the world a few hours ago. I don't know what it is, no one does, except maybe you and ... what did you say your name was?' he asked Daniel.

'I didn't,' replied Daniel, not bothering to be friendly.

Anton's eyebrows raised, but he shook off Daniel's surliness to focus on me. 'There are people on TV talking about the end of the world. They have all kinds of experts giving their viewpoint: politicians, religious leaders, supposed supernatural experts. The only one that made sense was a complete kook who said we were witness to demons wielding source energy and that they were going to return to take over the Earth soon. He said he had been a familiar to a demon for more than three hundred years. They kicked him off the show at that point.'

I kept my mouth shut, unsure what I could say or whether I should just tell him the truth. I settled for, 'You should get to wherever you were going and forget you saw me.'

I tried to move on, but he moved with me and he was arguing. 'But I want to help. Being a barman is okay for a job, but it's not exactly exciting. There's a bigger world out there and I want to see it.'

'Whoa, there, Anton. This isn't safe. You saw what the demons can do. They killed people here today.'

He countered my statement with, 'Worse is coming, right?'

I pulled a face. 'Probably.'

'We need to keep moving,' Daniel insisted, starting forward again even as I was trying to put Anton off and leave him behind.

'I know where Alex lives, anyway,' Anton told me, the subtext was a threat that he was going to follow me to her house no matter what I said.

I started walking. Daniel was right about the need to be elsewhere; it wasn't safe for me to be on the street. If I were spotted, the police would come for me and we would either have to travel between realms or fight them off. Neither thing appealed.

'You know, your picture is all over the news,' Anton told me as we hurried down a side street away from the main business district. 'I'm guessing you didn't kill your flatmate though.' He was saying these things as if it were a topic of conversation, but then his eyes flared, and his head snapped around to stare at me. 'Or was she a creature that you had to kill?'

I was still sad that Sarah had been killed and I felt responsible because I knew she would be alive if I hadn't been her flatmate. 'She was killed by demons. Wasn't she, Daniel?' I growled at him.

There was no sense in dwelling on her death, but I was conscious it occurred because Daniel had thought of me as a chess piece to manoeuvre. To manipulate me into allowing him to bind me, he'd sent a hit squad after me and then pretended to rescue me from them. They, of course, double crossed him and were working for Nathaniel. I didn't think remorse was an emotion that would occur to the demon walking by my side, but when I glanced at him, he wouldn't meet my eyes.

Alex lived on the other side of the ring road that ran along the side of the old cobbled High Street. A new train station had been built there a short while ago, and with it several new blocks of flats. She lived in one of them. It gave her the vibrant town just a short walk away, easy access to the coast or London via the train, and the library was just across the street. It would take only minutes to get to her place, not that I knew she was there, but Anton filled the journey with words.

'The thing you do with your hand, when you make light appear in it, does that hurt?' he asked. Then he wanted to know how I was able to make it and then switched his attention to speak directly to Daniel.

'Are you the same as Anastasia?' He stuck out his hand for the demon to shake. 'I guess you worked out that I'm Anton.'

Daniel looked down at Anton's hand and raised his own, but he didn't move to shake it, he pushed hellfire energy into his palm. Anton watched it with fascination and reached forward to touch the glowing orb.

I stopped suddenly, spinning off my back foot as I swung a punch with my left hand. The prosthetic carbon fibre limb connected with Daniel's face in the space between his left eye and nose. It rocked his head back and jarred my arm, hurting the stump.

Daniel stumbled backwards and the sword fell free from his jacket. Anton danced back a pace, shocked by what had happened, but I paid him no mind. I was watching the demon to see if he would be stupid enough to retaliate.

His head was facing down and away from me, but when he looked up, he was laughing. 'I wasn't going to let him touch it,' he chuckled.

I wasn't certain I believed him. Daniel had killed plenty of humans over many, many years – centuries probably. I doubted he cared about one more, or lots more. Like all demons, he thought himself above the mortal human race.

Daniel recovered, straightening back up to his full height, and some of his swagger had returned; the cockiness that had allowed him to advance in the demon hierarchy, for all the good it did him.

I reached down to collect the sword from the floor. I didn't know how delicate it was; probably not very was my guess since it had lasted thousands of years already, but it would be a terrible irony if I dropped it and broke it. With it held in my right hand, I slowly pushed power into it, making it light up from within. Behind me, Anton made a sound which might have been surprise or fright or something else. I didn't look his way; I was focussed on the demon.

'I only want to say this once, Daniel. I'm prepared to wipe the slate clean. Your past sins are not forgiven but I will not judge you by them now. I need you, and I think you need me. The death curse will fall, and they will come for you. They will come for you anyway, but your only hope of long-term survival is for humanity to win the coming fight. However, despite my belief that I need you to complete the task ahead, if you kill a human, I will end you.'

His mouth curled into a cocky expression and I knew he was going to say something clever which is why I swung the sword. The tip clipped his left cheek as I intended, drawing blood with a hiss as if scalded by a branding iron.

The cockiness left him instantly, and he jumped back, holding that side of his face in abject shock. I took fast steps forward now that he was off balance, making it look like I might just kill him for the hell of it. He stumbled and fell backward, landing on the pavement with his eyes wide.

I stopped by his feet; the sword held at my side but ready. 'What's that, Daniel?' I asked as if he had spoken. 'Suddenly remembered what it is like to be mortal? Terrifying, isn't it; the thought of dying? You will fight for me. You will help me find the other artefacts, or you have no purpose, and I will kill you.' I meant every word of it.

He looked wounded, not just the thin line on his face which oozed blood and refused to heal – the God sword is a wonderous thing - but his expression. 'I got you out of hell,' he protested, his voice a furious snarl that ought to have frightened me.

'You freed me so you could escape,' I snarled in return, not letting up on my harsh words and making sure he could see the sword was still powered. 'When I arrived, you were bound and lying on the ground at Beelzebub's feet. You are on the run from the demon horde and we only have each other. I will do this without you if I must, maybe I can find Otto Schneider,' I watched him tense at the mention of the wizard's name. 'I would rather you and I worked together.'

I eased back on the magic, allowing the source energy powering the sword to dwindle until the light inside went out. His gaze flitted between my eyes and the sword until I held out my left hand to help him up.

Once he was back on his feet, I did something that was either the winning move or the one which would get me killed: I gave him the sword back. Then, in a show of confidence, I turned my back on him and went to Anton.

I couldn't tell if Anton was scared or excited and I wasn't hanging around to find out. Grabbing his left elbow in my right hand, I started steering him toward the main road and beyond it to Alex's flat.

On the way, I growled some advice. 'That glowing red light is called hellfire. It kills mortals on contact. No living thing can survive it.'

'I saw you get hit with it earlier today,' he argued.

Good point.

'No living thing other than me, then. There is something special about me,' I heard him draw a breath to ask a question and rolled right over the top of it. 'Don't bother asking me what it is, I don't have the faintest idea. Just trust me when I say hellfire will kill you. Likewise, the sword. I saw it kill a man when he tried to pick it up. It tore through him like a million volts, lighting him up from the inside.'

'What is it?' he asked, his voice coming out as a hushed whisper.

I gave him the straight answer. 'The sword of God.'

My answer made his head spin around to see if I was being serious. 'Like, THE God?' he wanted to know.

I gave him a half shrug. I was still gripping his elbow and steering him onwards but stole a glance over my shoulder to see if Daniel was, in fact, following us. He was, the sword out of sight again inside his jacket, and his attention on the cut on his face. He'd been self-healing since the death curse started back when human history was in the bronze age. Having a cut that wouldn't heal must be quite a shock.

To give Anton a better answer while we waited for a break in the traffic, I said, 'God doesn't exist in the same way religion tells us. There was a supreme being, but he wasn't omnipotent, all seeing, and omnipresent, he was just magical and the most powerful of a race who dominated the Earth and ruled over mankind. I'll explain better when we have time, but for now, like the hellfire, just trust me and don't touch the sword.'

A double-decker bus went by, bland expressions on the faces of the people inside as they stared at the back of the head in front. After it, came a gap which allowed all three of us to jog across the road. We could have walked down to the traffic lights and the pedestrian crossing, but I could see people there, and according to Anton, my face was plastered all over the news. I did not need to get recognised now.

Once safely on the right side of the road for Alex's house, something Anton had said finally registered. 'How do you know where Alex lives?' I was asking him the question but also voicing what felt like an incongruity. He looked at me like I was being daft, and I blushed, letting go of his arm finally to cover my now open mouth. 'Oh, God, you two hooked up!'

Chapter 3

'No, I got drunk and he helped me get home!' cackled Alex when Anton let her know about my assumption. It made me blush again that he told her.

'I told you,' Anton bragged. He was right, of course. He denied it straight away, not that it was any of my business or even of interest. I wished my friend luck and figured it must be hard to pick up guys when you are over six feet tall and have a figure a polite person would call womanly or perhaps buxom. 'I delivered her safely home, made sure she was comfortable and let myself out,' Anton repeated for perhaps the third time.

'A perfect gentleman,' Alex commended him, then to me she whispered, 'More's the pity.'

We arrived on her doorstep just a few minutes ago, long enough for her to have put the kettle on but recent enough for the drinks to yet be served. She opened up as if expecting a takeaway order to be delivered, which it turned out was exactly what she thought we were. After a second's pause, in which she looked at me and then my two male companions, she lunged forward to grab me. Pulling me into a bear hug, she wrestled me inside her apartment and beckoned the guys to join us.

'I saw you on the news,' she announced, coming through to her living space from her small kitchen with a tray of steaming mugs. 'They are calling you a terrorist and claiming you blew up a police station. What happened to your flat mate?'

I stopped myself from looking Daniel's way. 'Demons killed her. They were looking for me.' I sipped the too hot coffee, savouring the flavour since it was the first anything to pass my lips in too many hours. 'Have you got anything to eat?' I begged. 'I'm honestly starving.' I knew she wanted answers to the questions that must be making a mad queue in her head, but I was beginning to feel faint from lack of sleep and food.

It was precisely at the pause in conversation that the doorbell rang, an angry buzzing sound that filled the room. Daniel's eyes found mine and he opened his jacket where he gripped the sword. He let it fall free, catching its pommel so he could offer it to me, and I could see the source energy filling his body as red sparks began to track across his chest.

'Calm down,' laughed Alex. 'It's just my takeaway delivery.' She bustled to the door, snagging her purse from a side table on the way. In her small apartment, I stood ready for her to be wrong, but she wasn't; not unless the demons outside were big on using props because she came back with a thin white plastic bag in which I could see hot-looking cartons. Quite a few of them.

She held the bag aloft as she made her way back to the kitchen. 'I won't say there's enough for everyone, but I always order enough to do a couple of meals and then freeze what I don't eat the first night.' It was Chinese food and my stomach growled loudly when the smell hit my nostrils.

I don't remember running to the kitchen, but I got there quick enough to startle Alex who was starting to pull bowls from a cupboard and chopsticks from a drawer.

'Can I get a fork?' begged Anton.

Alex let me get a forkful of hot, spicy noodles into my mouth, but then pressed me for information. 'Come on, midget,' I wasn't exactly keen on her nickname for me, especially since I hadn't adopted the one people used for her: big bird. I let it slide though. 'Spill the beans,' she demanded. 'What the hell is going on? Last week you had two wizards fighting over you, now it's demons? Your image is all over the internet – someone filmed you firing your light pulse from your hand in Rochester High Street and the world thinks you are a terrorist. Everyone but me, obviously.'

I swallowed my mouthful and scooped up another, opting to speak around my food rather than wait any longer to get it into my ravenous belly. 'No one knows what I am,' I mumbled. I glanced at Daniel because I couldn't very easily tell this story without making him the bad guy. He had barely spoken since I cut his face and threatened to kill him. He was behaving, but he wasn't happy about it and, truth be told, I wasn't sure where we stood. 'There are a few unique things about me that you don't know because I didn't know them either. I suspect there will be even more things that I am yet to find out, but I need your help.'

Alex's eyebrows made a bid for freedom. Her lips were pursed at the time as she sucked in a loose strand of noodle and it made her face look like a surprised coconut. 'My help? With what?' Before I could answer, she held up a hand to stop me. 'No, Ana. No skipping ahead. I want to know what happened yesterday and where you have been.'

I relented and told her everything that had happened since I last saw her. We worked together in the library. In different parts of it, doing different jobs, but she and I were friends already and had lunch together most days with a third girl, Abigail. After I left work two days ago, I heard the shilt attacking someone, met Daniel, fought him, went home, got attacked by different demons there ... it went on. I left out that Shaun McGuire, the wizard I killed last week, was sent by Daniel. I didn't trust the demon sitting across from me, and though I wanted both Anton and Alex to be wary of him, sitting around her table eating Chinese food wasn't the right time to regale them with his evil past.

I explained about retrieving the sword and fighting hordes of demons, about the fight outside Anton's pub, and meeting the ruler of hell. I finished bringing Alex up to speed with the bit where I plunged the sword through Nathaniel's chest. By then, both Alex and Anton were staring at me with open mouths while Daniel hoovered up all the food.

I shrugged at them. 'I figured I was about to die anyway. I might as well go out with a satisfied grin on my face.'

'But you didn't die,' Daniel pointed out, popping a prawn ball in his mouth, and moving it into his cheek so he could speak. 'The sword should have killed you. That it didn't is truly remarkable and that alone will make Beelzebub thoroughly nervous.'

He made it sound like a dread statement from a horror movie. The sort of line someone delivers right before the monster reaches into the room with a tentacle to grab a lesser member of the cast. No portentous flash of lightning illuminated the curtains, but I still jumped when Alex spoke.

'You said you needed my help,' she reminded me. 'How on Earth can a tall girl with a big bottom help against demons, wizards and ogres? You've got a magical hand cannon and you are carrying God's sword. I feel a librarian's excellent filing ability might be the wrong skillset for what you suggest is to come.'

I finished the final morsels in my bowl and wished I had a beer to chug, then I hit Alex with a broad grin. 'That's because I haven't told you the best part.' I looked at Daniel sitting opposite me. The cut on his face had stopped bleeding but it still wasn't healing. I wondered if that would prove to be a sore point between us. When I caught his eye, I said, 'You're up, stud.' I got a blank look in return. 'How many other artefacts are there?' I asked. It was a question I had wanted an answer to since I first learned there might be more than just the sword.

Was I the right person to hold them? I've got no idea how to answer that. What I knew was that I felt uncomfortable with anyone else getting them first given the potential power they held.

Daniel leaned back into his chair. Looking directly at me, he didn't answer straight away. I took his delay as a sign that he was trying to determine the best way to lie and nothing about his answer, when it finally came, changed my mind. 'I don't know.' I guess he saw the look of anger cross my face because he swiftly followed his first response up by saying. 'I'm not sure anyone does. You have to accept how long ago it was when anyone last saw these things.'

'Keep talking,' I insisted, but Alex interrupted.

'What are we talking about here?' She looked from me to Daniel and back to me. 'You said artefacts. Are we talking truly ancient, like they predate known human history?' Her eyes were wide and dilated like she was sexually aroused by the concept. She was a research assistant at the library, that was why I needed her. Or, at least, why I thought she would prove useful.

I pressed Daniel again. 'What else lies buried in the Earth's past? Is it more weapons?'

He shook his head, slowly left and right. 'A suit of armour. A helmet, a shield ... but, yes, there may also be other weapons. In my time before the death curse was levied and our world changed, I do not recall ever seeing the supreme being wear his armour or wield his sword. There was no need. His rule was benevolent: he had no enemies. The armour and weapons came from a different time. Our race was not always so peaceful. Until the supreme being's family became the dominant one, there were tribes and clans all fighting for the right to lead. It was only after the fighting stopped that the armour was forged. At least, that's what I remember being told. It was forged. It was used when challengers were foolish enough to stand against the supreme being, but the challengers dwindled swiftly when it became obvious they couldn't win. Legend has it that the armour made the wearer impervious to the magic of others, and the weapons ensured the supreme being would swiftly defeat anyone who stood against him.'

'Why is there only one?' Anton wanted to know. 'Why didn't challengers get their own suit of armour and magic sword?'

Daniel looked at the barman. 'It wasn't allowed.' We all waited for him to say more, but that was all he had to offer.

'A suit of armour,' I murmured, picturing the safety such a thing might provide. I might be able to wield the sword and kill demons. I was already able to absorb their hellfire which effectively nullified their primary weapon, but how long would it be before they got wise to that and used a different kind of weapon against me? I refocussed my attention on Daniel. 'Where is it?'

He gave me an apologetic face. 'I don't know that either.'

'You found the sword,' I growled at him.

My tone made him defensive. 'It took over two hundred years to track that down and I still wasn't sure I had the right location until you produced it. I have a few leads on where some of the other artefacts are, but I don't know if you will be able to use them even if we can find them.'

I looked him straight in the eye. 'Then we will destroy them. Both sides want the sword and the armour, that much I am sure of. I mean to introduce a third side. The demons and angels are coming back, that I accept. They expect to fight each other for dominion over the Earth, but they haven't factored in humanity.'

Daniel couldn't stop the smile from reaching his face. 'You think the humans can stand against my race?'

Feeling directly affronted, I went on the offensive. It was something I had been doing my entire life and it had rarely done me any favours. 'How many demons are there?'

I got a lazy shrug in reply. 'Twenty-five thousand maybe. The majority are congregated close to Beelzebub, but there are others who spread out, distancing themselves from the collective. The number is insignificant though.'

'How so?' I demanded through clenched teeth.

He shifted in his seat, leaning forward to place his elbows on the table as he continued to grin at me. 'You have armies, right?'

'Lots of them.'

'And they have tanks, and planes, and helicopters and stuff.'

'Yes.'

'And some of your nations have nuclear weapons, isn't that the name they came up with?'

'Yes.'

'All worthless,' he concluded. 'The magic Beelzebub plans to unleash will roll over the Earth in a way you cannot imagine. I never made it into his inner circle but there were rumours he has hordes of magical beasts ready for the invasion. Nuclear weapons will do nothing to a race who can conjure shields from the elements or open portals to move between places.'

I screwed up my face. 'I've never once seen a demon create a shield, only the wizards, and I thought your portals only moved between realms.'

Daniel flipped his eyebrows. 'Why would a demon raise a shield when they are immortal? You may have interfered with that theory in killing Nathaniel, but for millennia, it has been considered cowardly to hide behind a shield. As for the portals, it was always possible before the death curse to move between places on Earth. We assume that power will return when the curse falls.'

I considered what he said but it only strengthened my resolve. I asked a question that I had been wanting to ask for a while. 'Why are there no children?'

I got a look from Alex. 'No children?' she echoed.

Without taking my eyes from the demon, I explained my question, 'I went to the angels' camp and to demon HQ and I never saw one being who was younger than an adult. What happened to the children, Daniel?'

He sagged a little in his chair. 'There is wild speculation. There has been ever since the curse. When the supreme being died and we were torn from the Earth, we found ourselves in a parallel version of the mortal realm. You know this already,' he told me. 'What you don't know is that no one below the age of eighteen was with us.' He paused to let that sink in. 'We don't know where they went. Many assumed the supreme being left them on Earth. We were doomed to never age, but was it fair to do the same to the children? What would it be like to never grow if you are a baby?' He blew out a tired breath. 'Of course, others theorised that he couldn't leave them on earth, taking all the adults away would doom many of them to die. And still others believed he sent them somewhere else, to a place where they might grow up differently to those who went before. The point is the children didn't come to the immortal realm and no one knows what happened to them.'

'They stayed on earth,' I announced, making myself sound sure of the fact even though I wasn't. 'Maybe some did die, but those who survived grew up among mankind and were absorbed by them. The magic was bred out of them maybe, or perhaps the curse robbed them of their magic which is why the elder children didn't simply restart the demon community with them as leaders over the humans. I think they were suddenly without the ability to summon source energy and became one with the humans around them.' I was getting a sceptical look from all three of my companions. 'Think about it. The children were here on Earth four thousand years ago. The youngest ones would grow up never knowing they were any different. They look like us, and with the magic stripped away, they would be no different physiologically.'

Alex started to see what I was getting at. 'That's why magic is manifesting.'

Daniel shook his head in disbelief.

'Don't you see?' I argued. 'As the death curse weakens to allow the demons to push into the mortal realm, so too the magic buried inside humanity begins to surface. Where does my power come from? How can I wield source energy? It had lain dormant in humans for millennia, and now it is coming to life. What percentage of the planet can wield elemental magic if trained? How many others will prove to be like me?'

'None.' The demon shook his head again. He got what I was telling him, but he didn't want to believe it.

Alex, though, was all over my idea. She swivelled in her seat to grab her laptop from a sideboard behind her. 'There are wizards and werewolves and other creatures being reported all over the world. In the last twenty-four hours there has been a huge spike in reported incidents. Something huge happened in Berlin; a load of cops and civilians were killed, and the internet is lighting up with ...'

'I was there,' I admitted quietly. 'Beelzebub wanted to demonstrate his power to his brother. I was with the angels at the time but bound to one of Beelzebub's generals as his familiar.'

'His familiar,' Anton showed his confusion.

'Slave,' I explained, giving it a more accurate term. 'Beelzebub demanded I be returned to him and Godfrey refused, so the demons went on a rampage.' My voice was quiet when I murmured, 'I bet they killed thousands.'

Daniel didn't help my mood when he said, 'Whatever he did yesterday, is nothing compared to what will come when the curse falls.'

Alex turned her laptop around to show everyone footage taken at various sites around the world. The screen showed half a dozen different tiled squares and, in the bottom left, was Rochester High Street where a diminutive, doll-like character fired a bolt of light from her hand into the head of a demon called Ezekiel. I have always been surprised by just how small I look compared to everyone else around me. My proportions are childlike.

I had no reason to doubt Daniel's claims that the world was in for a tough time, but a plan was forming at the back of my head. 'Daniel, do Beelzebub's plans allow for the humans to resist with magic?'

I got a single raised eyebrow. 'No. Elemental magic, conjured by humans is insignificant and so few of you can use it, any resistance would be swept before us.'

'But what if there are more like me?' I asked.

He didn't get to answer because someone started hammering on Alex's front door.

Chapter 4

Beelzebub

In his chambers, the lord of the demons had problems to manage. He was managing one right now by pushing a sword through its chest.

'How long had Nathaniel been plotting against me?' he growled into his captive's face. The lesser demon was pinned to a wall by the sword a foot off the ground which placed its face at roughly the same height as Beelzebub. It couldn't be killed, but pain ... it could feel pain and it knew all about that subject right now.

The demon being tortured was Jerome, one of Nathaniel's senior aides. Many of Nathaniel's supporters chose to run the moment they saw him die. Now, disbelief was rife: those who hadn't seen it refused to believe it had happened, but there was no doubt in Jerome's mind. When the slip of a human girl plunged the sword through his master's chest and lit him up from within, Jerome had been standing no more than a few yards from the event.

Both Jerome's hands were on the blade of the sword as it stuck out from between his ribs. Not that he thought he could free himself, or that there was any point in doing so. He had backed the wrong horse and now he had to pay the price.

'I was deceived, my Lord,' he wheezed. 'We all were.' Jerome didn't care what happened to Nathaniel's other followers. Not really, but it occurred to him that he might do better if he made it look like Nathaniel had lied to them all. 'Nathaniel told us he was serving you. I believed his lies, sire. Why wouldn't I? He has been your trusted lieutenant for my entire existence.'

'When he openly challenged me, you rallied behind him,' Beelzebub pointed out calmly.

Jerome shuddered, the pain of his wounds making it hard to speak. 'I was confused, my Lord. I would never stand against you. Never.' Jerome was lying through his clenched teeth. He had seen opportunity with Nathaniel. The humans would fall when the demons returned; that much they all knew, so it became a question of who got the greatest share of the Earth and its bounty. Who would have the best of it, the most servants, or the greatest respect? He could never be the leader, but he could back the one who would be. For Jerome, that had been Nathaniel, and it had already proven to be a costly wrong choice.

Beelzebub leaned in close to Jerome's face. 'How long? How long had you been plotting against me?' he demanded, his face close enough that Jerome could feel the warmth of his breath.

'I wasn't, Sire, I swear. None of us knew Nathaniel's true intentions. I didn't even know about the girl.' That part was actually true. 'We all remember your father's sword and armour but none of us knew Nathaniel was attempting to retrieve it. Even when he appeared with the sword, I thought he intended to present it to you as a token of fealty.'

Beelzebub was bored of listening to Jerome's senseless chattering. He didn't believe what he was being told, and if half of it were true, then Jerome and the rest of Nathaniel's followers were dumber than dirt and deserved what he now planned for them.

With a grunt, he gripped the sword and pulled it free from the wall. Jerome fell free, collapsing in a heap until Beelzebub nodded his head at two demons waiting at the periphery of his chambers. They yanked Jerome roughly to his feet and spun him around to face the demons' leader.

Beelzebub's command was an easy one, but the last thing Jerome expected to hear. 'Take him to the pit.'

Horrified, the lesser demon screamed his distress. 'No, master! I beg you! I have wronged you; I see that now, but my heart has always been yours.'

Beelzebub held up a finger to stay the demons taking Jerome away. For a brief second, the demon hanging limply from their arms felt a ray of hope. Until Beelzebub spoke, that is. 'Cut out his heart and let him carry it into the pit with him.'

When the echoes of Jerome's screams faded, the leader of the race who would soon rule the Earth left the room. Waiting within earshot were four more demons: four of his remaining generals. The fifth one was absent, but the task he had for them was not a task for her. The three males and one female were all physical specimens, frozen in the prime of their lives by the death curse. Before they were trapped in the immortal realm, they were already four of Beelzebub's most loyal followers. They each believed wholly in his right to lead their race to dominion over the Earth and knew they would be the ones delivering his battle plans.

Today though, he had a different task for them.

'You want us to go after her?' asked Martha, the lone female of the group. Though she was more than four millennia old, her appearance was that of a gym-toned woman in her late twenties. Her dark brown hair had been pulled tight into a braid which was then pinned to her head.

Beelzebub smiled at his generals. 'Do you feel up to the task?'

Bitrius, a demon who would be identified as Eritrean were he on Earth given his dark skin and facial bone structure, sniggered and hefted a cruel-looking axe. 'It has been a while since I hunted a human. I doubt it will be any different this time from the last.'

'She killed Nathaniel with ease just a short while ago,' pointed out a third member of the foursome. Aksel was well-known as the most cautious of their team but he made a valid point. 'She then killed four more when they went after her.'

'They went after the sword,' argued Martha. 'It hardly matters though. Nathaniel didn't see the danger that we now know she presents. Armed with that, killing her, and retrieving the sword will be easy. She is just a human.'

Aksel shook his head. 'She is something more than human. If we are less than wary, she may get the better of us too.'

His comment got three snorts of derision, and a disbelieving face from Martha that suggested he had just made a joke. 'You know what the humans call us, don't you?'

Aksel didn't think it was funny it at all. 'That is just a legend that we have bent to fit our circumstances.'

'It's still true, Aksel,' Bitrius placed a hand on his companion's shoulder but it was intended to be mocking, not comforting. 'We are the four horsemen of the apocalypse. Where we ride, death and destruction will follow.'

Refusing to let his peers annoy him, Aksel nevertheless shook off Bitrius's hand as he replied with a question. 'How do you propose to kill her, brother? She absorbs hellfire. Is she immortal?'

The only one of the four yet to speak was Acadus, and he chose that moment to roar with laughter. 'Immortal? Did you not see that she is terribly scarred and missing parts of her body? If hellfire will not kill her, I'm willing to bet cutting off her head will.' He hefted a gleaming black blade to emphasise his point.

Beelzebub interrupted their flow and ruined Acadus's plan. 'I want her alive.'

All four of his general's stopped arguing to look at their master.

Martha was first to speak, 'That's going to make things a lot harder.'

'That is why I am sending you and not entrusting this task to lesser demons. Have you considered that she may attempt to get more of my father's relics?' Beelzebub's great height allowed him to stare down at everyone in his realm, a tactic he employed every chance he got. He employed it now, holding the gaze of each demon present for a second to let his words sink in. 'She may or may not be able to heal from wounds now even though she clearly could not when her terrible injuries were inflicted. What we do know, is that she is able to use my father's sword. I intend to find out how that is possible and for that I need her alive.' He paused again, looking at his subordinates before continuing. 'We do not know when the curse will fail or what might happen when it does, but wisdom suggests that we will all be thrust back into the mortal realm as the two worlds become one again. We cannot know when that will happen and therefore, we must be ready. Nathaniel's treachery weakened us, but that we can recover from. Imagine if this tiny human girl is not alone in her ability to wield source energy.' Again, he paused to let his words sink in. 'If Daniel chooses to help her find the armour, will she be able to wear it? Imagine the same tiny human girl wearing my father's armour and wielding his sword. Would any of you wish to face her alone?'

The four horsemen exchanged glances, tendrils of doubt beginning to creep in as they joined Aksel in viewing the girl as a threat.

Beelzebub, a master at delivering the right words at the right time, said, 'Go now. Find her and bring her to me. I will dissect her if it proves necessary, for we must know what she is and how she can channel source energy without burning up. If Daniel is still with her, do what you want to defeat him, and bring his pieces back to me. I believe he will prove to be the key to tracking her down. He will leave traces as he travels to stay ahead of the sun. Now that he is on the run, I think he will go after the armour - use that to trap them both.'

'Sire, we do not know where the angels hid it,' complained Martha.

Beelzebub nodded, but swept the concern away as if trifling. 'Nor do the angels, I believe, and yet Daniel was able to find the sword. The armour will have been broken up and distributed across the Earth. I doubt they can obtain it without leaving a mess behind. Follow that and you will be able to find them.'

No further words were needed. They had their mission, a mission entrusted to them by their ruler, the most powerful of their race. Aksel took a step backwards to get a little space, and there he opened a portal. Holding out his free hand for the other three to touch, they went through together.

The room became suddenly silent leaving Beelzebub to contemplate the magnitude of the task ahead. He would never reveal his thoughts, but the ability of the girl truly worried him. A small noise brought his attention around to a doorway from which his remaining general emerged.

Berthilda was older than her comrades, and though not so old as Nathaniel had looked, she stood apart from the other four because she had lines on her face and grey in her hair. While the others bickered and joked, she had listened. Beelzebub viewed her skillset as different from the others and always had. She led an army for him because she was capable of thinking strategically, but she was not a ruthless fighter like so many of her kind.

She approached the ruler of her race curious to hear what tasks he might have for her.

Chapter 5

The sudden noise at Alex's door made three of us jump. Only Daniel showed no sign of surprise. Alex and I glanced at each other as the hammering continued. It was loud, urgent, and insistent.

I didn't bother to ask if she were expecting company; I could tell from her face that she was not. Instead, I grabbed the sword and barked at Daniel. 'We're going to need a portal.' Turning to face the threat, I kept the sword in my left hand and drew in source energy to power sinfire in my right. A glowing light blue orb appeared at my silent command, but I don't know if it was that, or the grimace on my face that made Anton back away, but he was out of his chair and keeping it between us in a heartbeat.

This was my fault. Too tired to consider strategy, I had gone for the first place of refuge I could think of. I needed Alex to help me locate the artefacts, and because I desperately wanted to not feel quite so alone in this fight. But coming to her flat had been stupid. There was one way in and out; a single door which we were now trapped behind.

Daniel ought to have been conjuring a way out, but he came to stand beside me. 'Demons don't knock,' he said calmly.

His valid point made me panic yet more. The demons I felt ready to deal with; I could unleash on them with no concern, but if it were not the demons, it had to be the police.

'Anastasia!' a voice shouted from outside. I knew that voice. 'Miss Aaronson, its's Detective Sergeant Spencer! Open the door! You've got to get out of here right now!'

I took a fast step forward and then stopped. Was this a trap? Would they use him to lure me outside so they could take me down with minimal danger to themselves? 'Are you alone?' I shouted back. I didn't know how he knew I was here, but I was nervous about opening the door.

'Yes, Gods dammit! The police are coming and that other bunch – the SIA. You've got less than a minute!'

I swore loudly. So much for taking refuge and recuperating. Alex shoved rudely by me, knocking my shoulder on her way to the door. 'I don't want the police in here wrecking the place,' she whined. 'I just had the carpets cleaned.

Beside me, Daniel readied hellfire in both his hands and, for once, I didn't discourage him, but I did growl, 'Don't shoot anyone unless I say so.'

I got side eye from him. 'You trying to control me is going to get boring really fast, Anastasia.'

As Alex opened the door, I replied, 'Get used to it.'

DS Spencer tumbled through the door, but he didn't try to get inside, he merely hovered on the welcome mat, his eyes wide. 'Seriously, we've got to go. They can't be more than a minute behind me.' He was beckoning for me to leave and there was no doubting the urgency in his voice and actions.

Whether he was leading me into a trap or not, the danger that he was telling the truth was too great to ignore. Swearing again, I rushed forward.

'Come on, Daniel!'

'I'll tell them you were never here!' shouted Alex as I got to the door. 'Anton and I can make it look like we are just a couple making out on the sofa.' She moved toward him, untucking her top as she went.

'Say what now?' asked Anton, looking not only confused but also a little scared of my friend as she advanced on him with lust in her eyes.

DS Spencer stopped her. 'They know Miss Aaronson is here because they are watching the place and have it bugged. They will arrest you the moment they arrive,' he promised.

'My flat is bugged!' Alex screeched, though truly, I thought she was more upset about not being able to fake make-out with the barman.

Then it was too late for anything, as multiple cars began to peel off the main road and into the carpark below at speed. DS Spencer swore. I swore. But Daniel merely sauntered up to the edge of the railings outside Alex's front door. Looking down, he lifted his hands above his head, forming hellfire orbs in each palm.

'May I?' he enquired though he wasn't really asking me and would have started blasting whoever it was in the cars below if I hadn't jabbed him in the gut. My needle-sharp elbow spoiled his aim, the two blasts of red death smashing harmlessly into the tarmac.

It did a good job of scaring whoever was in the cars. They stopped instantly as drivers slammed on their brakes, and the people inside bailed out. The cars were all unmarked and the men and women charging toward the building all wore civilian clothes. That they were cops or SIA was not in question but seeing the guns in their hands came as a surprise.

'Portal now!' I barked. I could have taken Daniel and escaped, but DS Spencer had information that might prove useful: like where we could go and not find ourselves being watched and how I could avoid the police altogether. I grabbed the detective's right jacket sleeve, yanking him along as I pushed Daniel back toward Alex's front door. 'Alex, I need you!' I shouted inside.

'Just getting my shoes!' she shouted back. 'Oh, my gosh, are we going through one of those portal things?'

Anton's bewildered face appeared right behind her as she ran to join me.

'We all have to be touching to shift through it!' I yelled, finding myself caught up in the intense adrenalin of our latest situation. 'Flesh to flesh!' I grabbed for Alex's hand and saw her grabbing for Anton's.

'We can't leave him behind to face the police alone!' she protested.

The air behind Daniel shimmered just as Alex closed her front door.

'I shouldn't bother,' said DS Spencer. 'They're going to break it down anyway.'

'Really?' Alex squeaked.

He nodded sadly. 'Miss Aaronson is a wanted terrorist right at the top of the list. They will go through your flat like a tornado. Your best bet is to stay here and talk to them.'

If she wanted to do that, she didn't get a chance because Daniel yanked my hand and we all went through the portal.

Chapter 6

It is perhaps a statement about how messed up my last week has been that I thought nothing about travelling through a portal to land in a place that the locals colloquially referred to as Hell. The odd sensation that accompanies the shift between realms can best be described as a momentary bout of indigestion as if one's body feels gassy for a half second. It is so fleeting that I have learned to ignore it.

'What the hell just happened?' gibbered DS Spencer. A second ago, we were standing on the gangway outside Alex's flat. We were way above ground level and in a jungle of concrete and high-rise apartments with a train going by less than a hundred yards away. Now we were standing in a dark clearing in a forest.

The moon was high above us, illuminating our faces so I could see the panic on DS Spencer's face. I still had hold of his right wrist with my right hand. Alex was holding his left which left him trapped between us, but there was no time to answer his question because Daniel was already opening another portal.

The demon's free hand, the one not conjuring the crossing between realms, was touching my neck, so when the gateway coalesced, he pulled me through and the five of us travelled again. I knew he would do this; he wouldn't want to spend any more time in the immortal realm than was absolutely necessary. Not that he was safe from the demons in the mortal realm, but that was where we needed to be to obtain the artefacts.

I hadn't had a chance to even give thought to where he might take us. I might have steered him or demanded where I wanted to go if I had been less tired and more alert, but coming through the portal, there was little question about where we were.

'I don't believe it,' whispered Anton, staring at the skyline reaching toward the stars. A yellow cab went by, the driver silently staring forward through his windscreen. If he had seen the portal open at the edge of the dark street, then he chose to pay it no mind. Maybe he had seen it all before.

'Why here?' I asked the demon.

Daniel released his hold on my neck just as I let DS Spencer go, but the middle-aged British policeman was struggling to comprehend what he was seeing. 'But,' he managed to get a single word out. 'But.'

'Why New York?' the demon asked. 'They make really good pastrami sandwiches and because I'm convinced there is at least one artefact here.'

'We're in New York,' Anton chuckled, overwhelmed by the idea to the point that it was making him laugh. 'I just teleported to New York in the company of a sword wielding pixie and a demon.'

'I'm not a pixie, thank you,' I frowned at him.

He stopped laughing. 'I thought you said you don't know what you are.'

I had to concede those were my exact words. 'I'm still not a pixie. There is no such thing,' I stated. Then, to Daniel, from the corner of my mouth, I asked, 'Is there?'

He was already moving away. 'I need coffee,' he called over his shoulder. 'If we are going on a quest for the armour – I've heard worse ideas – then I need to be fuelled and ready.' He didn't hang about to gauge my opinion or that of anyone else; he was leaving us behind if we didn't go with him.

Anton and Alex were looking to me for guidance and poor DS Spencer just looked lost. I grabbed the older man's hand, tugging him forward to make him follow me. 'Whatever else,' I said to my friends, 'Daniel is our ride. It would be best to keep up with him.' I also agreed with his thoughts on coffee, and despite the Chinese food I finished eating less than ten minutes ago, the idea of a pastrami sandwich really appealed.

I hadn't eaten much the last few days, okay?

With DS Spenser bumbling along by my side, I was hurrying to catch up with Daniel when Alex said, 'Don't you think you ought to hide the sword if we are going inside a place with other people?'

Cripes. I'd just about forgotten I had it in my left hand. I needed to find a sheath or a bag big enough to hide it in or the police here would soon be after me as well.

Anton caught up to me. 'All you need are some steampunk accessories, and no one will blink twice at the sword.'

'You mean like a costume?' I tried to confirm.

'Yeah. You know what steampunk is, right?'

I shook my head. 'Not really.' I turned to Alex. 'Give me your coat.'

I got a wide-eyed look. 'You want my coat?' I waggled the sword at her to show why I wanted it. 'Right, of course. Here.' She swished if from her shoulders as we emerged from one street to join a busier one and before we ran into people, I had the sword tucked safely out of sight.

Daniel was crossing the street ahead of us where a diner's illuminated sign announced Henri's Deli. I could see people inside: staff serving food from behind a counter, and customers sitting at tables. The place was packed.

Anton was fiddling with his phone, trying to find pictures to show me, I guessed, but Daniel was already going through the door, holding it open for the rest of us to follow and I caught a waft of the air from inside. I think I floated the final few feet and over the threshold, buoyed up by the incredible smells.

My arm got nudged by Anton as we paused for Daniel to get a table. Anton's phone was held so I could see the screen which displayed a young woman wearing a burgundy bowler hat with a lace fringe and a matching flock coat with lots of silver buttons. A monocle hung from her left lapel and the accessories didn't stop there. 'Steampunk is a fringe genre of science fiction, which can be set in the future on a different planet, but the technology is generally steam power and the clothing is Victorian England with advances and weapons.' I accepted his explanation, but I wasn't about to rush out and buy a new wardrobe just so the sword looked at home on me.

Daniel got a ticket and led us to a table. This was all very lovely, especially compared to the nightmare of the last few days of being shot at and chased, but Daniel said there might be an artefact in this city, and I needed to know more about that.

'Which artefact?' I pressed him the moment he paused. We were in a queue to order food, standing at the high counter where men of varying ages were landing steaming huge joints of beef which they then carved multiple slices from. My stomach gurgled at me despite my insistence that we had more pressing tasks.

With his eyes on the large board displaying the food options, Daniel turned his head slightly to speak over his shoulder. 'Might be a breast-plate. Might be a greave. Might be nothing. I was able to establish that it probably wasn't the sword and that ended my interest. Now, if we are going to try to collect it all, this seemed like as a good a place to start as any. I knew it would be just dark here.'

Daniel couldn't stay in the daylight in the mortal realm. Like almost everything else about the death curse, none of it was explained. No one seemed to know why some things were the way they were, but demons couldn't be in sunlight and they couldn't set foot on holy ground – of any denomination. Mosques, temples, churches, they all had the same effect which was to swiftly drain them of all their power and energy. They would die if they stayed too long, though since they were immortal, they would then come back to life when taken outside again.

'What's a greave?' I asked.

Alex answered for him. 'The part that covers the lower leg; the shin and calf.' Hardly exciting if that was what it was, but like Daniel said, if we were going to try to get them all …

The queue in front of us shifted and it was our turn. While Daniel ordered sandwiches, which would make up for the small portions we got from Alex's Chinese supper, I made sure DS Spencer was all right.

'How are you holding up?' I asked him. His eyes were darting around the room and there wasn't much colour in his face. I shook his arm to get his attention, his eyes shifting wildly to look down at mine. 'Spencer. How are you doing? Are you okay?'

'Okay?' he echoed almost robotically. 'I'm in New York, aren't I?' he stated.

'Yes. I need to thank you for alerting me to the police and SIA. Why did you do that?' He was the first police officer I met in Rochester, just hours after arriving in the city and not long after everything started to go supernaturally sideways. He decided instantly that I was guilty of something and started hounding me. It went on for more than a week until he got to arrest me for the murder of my flatmate, Sarah. Our first encounter felt like a lifetime ago now, but somehow was only eleven or twelve days ago. I wasn't sure what time zone I was in to know what the date was, but it hardly mattered. The point is, he found me after I fought and killed two shilt, but by then I was in the company of a person on whom the shilt had been feeding and ... let's just say he found me suspicious and everything I did after that just made him believe he was right. Now, I guess he thought differently.

He was staring at me with a dumb expression. 'I saw what you did. I saw what the other people did. I saw what happened to the verger when he touched that sword. I thought you were the problem, but the things that are happening ... what I saw on the news last night, it defies explanation and it terrifies me. You told me you were innocently standing by, but I get the impression you are at the centre of it.'

I blew out a frustrated breath and nodded glumly. 'I seem to be.'

He blew out a breath too, his expression unreadable. 'I monitored the investigation because I knew they were going to throw everything at it. Explosions, unexplained light shows, dead people, some of whom the coroner couldn't determine cause of death ... those things make people twitchy. They want you in custody so they can show they have done something about the death and destruction. I knew they would come for you the moment you were spotted, but I didn't know if that would result in a load more police getting killed or if the SIA would show up. Above all, I think I will feel happier if you are not in custody.'

Daniel turned around and thrust a plate in my direction. 'I assume a Rueben is acceptable.'

I looked down at the fat sandwich on the plate. It was two inches high, there was heat coming off it, and there were spears of pickles on the side. 'What's a Reuben?' I asked, lifting the plate to inspect it critically.

He handed plates out to everyone else, pushing us toward our table as he gathered the coffee. 'Right, who's paying?' he asked. We all looked at him. 'What? You think we use money in the immortal realm?'

I knew I wasn't going to pay because I didn't have any money. I didn't have any cards, a purse, or even a phone.

Mercifully, the demon was messing with us, producing a huge wad of notes from a pocket. 'Human money … it's such an odd concept. I picked this up a while ago.' He looked to have several thousand dollars in his hand.

I grabbed Alex's plate, nudging her towards the till. 'Can you sort him out before he draws any more attention our way, please?'

It might have been my first ever Reuben sandwich, but it wasn't going to be my last, not if I got my way. The flavours were sublime, and famished still, I fell upon it with my eyes closed. I was several bites in when I looked up to find Alex, Anton, and DS Spencer all staring at me.

Alex articulated their thoughts. 'Anastasia what is the plan?' She shifted her coffee cup around but didn't pick it up to take a drink. 'I mean, the world is in turmoil.' She looked around. 'Not that you would know it sitting here. Is there something you can do to make things better? Or are we just clutching at straws. Somehow, we are in a New

York deli eating sandwiches and party to a quest you have embarked upon. I want to say that I am with you … I just don't know what it is I am with you to do.' She stared down at her coffee again, and then back up before I could clear my mouth. 'Also, the police want you on some serious charges. They probably want me too now by association.'

'They will,' DS Spencer assured her.

'That means I can't go home, and I can't go to work,' she added.

DS Spencer looked morose when he chipped in, 'My car is in the carpark outside the house. The tracker on it will tell the police I was there, and they already had me on a warning because I reported what I saw outside the cathedral. They thought I was having some kind of mental break. I have to wonder what they think now, but they will guess that I was there to warn you.' He met my eyes. 'I'm stuck on team Anastasia whether I want to be or not. It feels like the end of the world. Is that what this is?' His question wasn't aimed at me, he was looking directly at Daniel when he said it.

Daniel cleared his mouth, running his tongue around his gums before opening his mouth. 'No, it's not the end of the world. Just the end of humans thinking they rule the planet.'

He got suitable gasps and gaping mouths from the three humans sat at the table, but not from me; I'd heard it all before.

'What does that mean to you?' I demanded to know. Daniel was beginning to piss me off. He had been meek and ready to help me just a few hours ago. However, his cockiness was returning now that we were away from the demons who would take him apart, and I didn't like it. 'If humanity falls, you will spend the rest of your life hiding from the demons,' his smile failed. 'You may think that you stand above us. You may want to believe you are something different and apart, but you're not. Not now. You better pray I can come up with a way to stop the demon horde. Or that someone can, because if we don't, they will come for you as much as they will anyone else. You helped me escape with the sword, but your good favour was burned out long before that.'

He knew it was true. I knew it was true. I didn't much care whether he liked it or not. My mouth was dry, and I could feel myself shaking with the tension I felt, but to show how together I was, I kept eye contact with him and lifted my sandwich to take a bite.

It was all on him now. He either fell into line, and stopped being a dick, or I had to go at this thing alone somehow.

In typical Daniel style, he brushed over what had just gone. 'The first artefact, hopefully, is in a cathedral in lower Manhattan. We should finish up here and try to get it, right?'

Chapter 7

The SIA

At the Supernatural Investigation Alliance's headquarters in London, Commissioner Michael Swinton listened to the report from his agents deployed in London with increasing disappointment. Magic was manifesting. That was the term renegade wizard, Otto Schneider, used and it seemed to fit. New supernatural players were appearing constantly. It was making his head swim just trying to keep tabs on them all. Many could be identified as insignificant, but reassuring himself, and those above him that was the case each time, was yet another drain on his resources.

Also according to Otto Schneider, the young woman the wizard rescued just a little more than a week ago, went on to kill a wizard and an ogre and, in his words, was something he had never seen or heard of before. She could use magic like a demon, yet she was human. Foolishly, Swinton had written words to that effect in his report on the incident in Rochester and immediately got back orders to drop everything non-essential and find her.

If only committing resources to it were guaranteed of a result. According to the very few witnesses his agents had been able to find, the woman, who several described as a girl, vanished through a portal. Not that the witnesses used the word portal, and nor would Swinton if it were not the standard term the Alliance had now adopted for the gateways the demons and angels used.

Having vanished, alarmingly not at her will if the witnesses were to be believed, she could be anywhere, so how was he supposed to find her? He did what he would with any other suspect and placed observation posts to watch her close friends and family. Fortunately, the young woman didn't appear to have many, and they got a hit within hours.

Now though, he had to report she slipped away before his agents could grab her. His boss, President Colt Ironbolt, (not THE president, though he acted as if he were) would ask how she could have escaped given that Swinton had agents close enough to be able to report it was her. Swinton knew Ironbolt would know what had happened, and he would have to admit he'd bungled things. He insisted the chaps on the ground wait for backup, but that gave the local police, who he should have known would be watching the same people, the time to move as well.

He would get shouted at probably. That he could handle. What irked him was having to start over again and that he'd already made the decision to involve Otto Schneider.

If he could get hold of him.

No sooner had he given thought to the idea that getting the wizard to do his bidding for a change might be insurmountable, he questioned if indeed he might not be able to deal with this internally. He had his own resources after all. His two shifters were capable individuals and Swinton believed they had connections within the supernatural community. They couldn't move around like the wizard, but then the wizard could move between realms and no one else seemed to be able to do that.

So yes, he would bring Otto Schneider into play if he could. When the wizard refused to play ball, Swinton would at least be able to demonstrate that the person Ironbolt believed to be 'the great hope' in their fight against the coming war, wasn't the team player he thought. Otto was undoubtedly off trying to track down more of his precious familiars.

In the meantime, Swinton called for Crockett and Tubbs. That wasn't their real names, obviously. It was just what Swinton continually called them because they refused to wear socks plus one was white and the other black. The lack of socks was something to do with their shifter nature - they wore as few clothes as they could reasonably get away with. Of course, he used the name of the two stars of Miami Vice as a joke, but being older than ninety-five percent of his staff, very few even got the joke and those that did, didn't bother to laugh.

Recruit the girl Ironbolt demanded. Sure, how hard can that be?

Chapter 8

G etting to the cathedral of St Patrick on 5th Avenue was easy enough. It wasn't even very far to go though I will tell you it is cold in New York in November. It is busy too.

The deli was on East Houston Street and we had come through the portal in a side street just around the corner from it. We had to walk about ten blocks, but with each one the traffic just got heavier. It was late afternoon, Daniel assured me, though Alex and Anton had a discussion about relative times between England and the US East coast and worked out that it had to be coming up on six in the evening. It was late November and the sun was down: in my head that sounded about right.

It was my first time in New York. Or, at least, I thought it was. The tiny piece of shrapnel that tore into my brain was kind enough to rip out my memory. According to the doctors, I was lucky the damage wasn't far worse since I could not only form new memories but also remember how to do everything. I just couldn't tell if I had ever been to Disney World as a kid or who I lost my virginity to. Or when. In fact, now I was thinking about it, I couldn't remember ever having sex. How depressing is that?

I wasn't dressed to be out in the cold in late November. Even fortified by a belly full of food, I was getting cold. There just isn't enough of me to keep the cold at bay and my jeans stretchy top and hoody were not doing the trick. In contrast, while I hugged myself and tried to keep the sword out of sight, my companions looked fine. Alex and Anton even seemed to be enjoying themselves.

It was DS Spencer who noticed my plight. 'Miss Aaronson, you look half frozen.' He was taking his own coat off, a shabby, ill-fitting trench coat in a light fawn colour. Beneath it, he had a jacket, shirt, and tie to keep the cool air at bay. I took the offered garment gladly, not least because it meant I had somewhere to hide the sword.

The coat stank of cigarettes, as did DS Spencer. With it wrapped around me, the body heat it contained from being on him, began to warm my skin. 'Thank you, Ralph.' I said. I got a raised eyebrow from him in return. 'What?' I asked with a chuckle. 'You didn't think I would remember your first name? How about if you stop calling me Miss Aaronson like you are about to arrest me, huh? We are kind of in this together now.'

'In this together?' he repeated. 'How do we even get out of it? I mean, it's not like I can go to an airport and book a flight back to England. I don't have my passport, for a start.'

I pointed out something he had failed to consider. 'You do have a good alibi for the police if they want to accuse you of alerting me to their presence though.'

He was startled by the idea. 'I guess you are right. I couldn't have done it: I was in New York. I might have to book into a hotel just to make sure my presence here is recorded.'

'There you go,' I patted his shoulder. It was the first time I had seen him smile since we arrived.

His smile didn't last long. 'Of, course,' he muttered. 'That might work on the police, but those goons from the SIA seem to know a lot more than they are letting on. They appeared in Rochester too fast after the rumpus at the castle. They had to have prior knowledge that it was going to happen.'

How could that be true? I didn't vocalise my question because Alex spotted the cathedral. It sat ancient and brooding amid high rise blocks which might have been accommodation or offices. They rose all around us, reaching for the sky to blot out the stars. The cathedral might have been the biggest building around when it was erected, but it certainly wasn't now. It was illuminated by spotlights in the ground, all aimed at the structure to show it off at night. The plaza to the front as we approached was littered with people: tourists taking in the sights. The cathedral was still open, I could see, more tourists coming in and out of the wide doors between the two towering spires.

Daniel stopped on the pavement, or should that now be sidewalk? I pondered, remembering my terminology. We were on the opposite side of the street with a view directly inside the tall building. 'This is as close as I get,' he stated, backing up to the burger joint behind him where he angled his right foot backward to lean against the wall, then changed his mind. 'I need new clothes,' he announced, pulling out a handful of notes again.

A steady stream of cars went by, and people too, a mix of tourists and locals, no doubt, each with purpose in their stride. New York was busy, vibrant and noisy. Too noisy for me to want to spend much time here.

Because he stopped, we all stopped, taking a pause before taking the next step. Alex bore a confused frown. 'Aren't we going in?' she asked. 'I thought that was what he brought us to New York for.'

'We are going in. He's not,' I told her. 'Demons do not do well with religious places.'

Anton eyed the demon quizzically. 'Would he burst into flames?'

'No. Look it doesn't matter. I don't need him. If the artefact is in there, we can retrieve it without him. There will be a marker on the wall. I hope there is anyway. That is what they had in Rochester where I found the sword. A marker on the wall above one in the floor.'

DS Spencer chose to join in. 'It wasn't easy to get to though,' he reminded me. It was something of an understatement. Until the verger arrived and showed us how to move the pews, we had been looking for a lever to force them to move, or perhaps a sledgehammer to smash our way down to the stone floor.

His comment reminded me of something else though. 'The verger knew about the sword.' I was facing the others with my back to the cathedral and I was backing toward the edge of the sidewalk. 'Maybe we can just ask,' I suggested, hopefully.

I got a few odd looks from the humans facing me, but no one argued. Just before I turned around to find a crossing, I caught Daniel's eyes again.

'I'll be right here,' he assured me. Then, seeing the question in my eyes, he asked, 'Where else would I go? I don't have to like it, but I am stuck with you. I'll buy new clothes and be back here before you know it.'

I accepted his statement at face value and pushed along to the nearest pedestrian crossing point. It was a four-way signal at a crossroads. I had warmed a little with DS Spencer's coat around me, but I hoped the church was heated inside. My breath was forming clouds above my head just like everyone else's to show how cool the air around us was.

The lights changed, an orange 'walk' sign illuminating or rather the 'Don't' bit extinguished, and people on both sides of the street set off like greyhounds from a trap, jostling for space in their bid to get to wherever they were going.

Approaching the cathedral entrance, I began to feel nervous. It was inexplicable since I was about to enter one of the few places I could reliably relax. The demons, and the angels for that matter, could not come in after me, so I was safe unless the demand for my arrest had gone international.

'Do we just find a guide?' asked DS Spencer.

I shook my head. 'No. Maybe a priest. I doubt a guide will know if they have an ancient artefact buried under the floor.'

'Maybe we should try to find the marker first,' suggested Alex. 'What does it look like?'

It was a good question, and one I hadn't thought to consider until she vocalised it. 'The one in the cathedral in Rochester was ...' I looked about for a pen or something I could use to draw with.

Sensing what I needed; Alex rummaged in her handbag. 'Here,' she offered me her phone with a freehand drawing screen loaded.

I repeated the symbol from Rochester as carefully as I could using the index finger of my right hand. It was wobbly and not exactly accurate, but they got the idea. I sucked on my teeth. 'Of course, I don't know that it will look like that at all,' I admitted. 'The one in Rochester was way up above my head and directly above one marked in the floor.'

Anton shrugged. 'I guess we split up and see what we find. Meet back here in fifteen minutes unless one of us finds it?'

'We should exchange numbers,' said Alex, taking her phone back and stepping in close to Anton again. It said a lot about her love life, or lack thereof, that Alex saw tonight as a chance to make a move on the barman. Whether he was aware of her forwardness and ignoring it, or just blissfully unaware, I couldn't tell, but I felt there were too many more pressing issues for my attention right now to worry about whether the two of them hooked up at some point.

I didn't have a phone, something I might need to change if I got a chance, but I also had no money and no way to access a bank either so it might be a moot point. Perhaps I should speak to Daniel about the wad of money he carried.

We split, dividing the huge church into chunks, and taking one each. I didn't watch as the others moved away, only catching an impression of them walking along with their faces looking upwards in contrast to everyone around them.

The cathedral was vast inside, the ceiling stretching up to a point so far above my head any detail there was lost to my eyes. Stained-glass windows sat above two rows of ornate columns that ran along both sides and there were yet more of the windows at each end. The detail was difficult to make out and only visible at all because the darkness outside was being beaten back by the floodlights illuminating the outer architecture.

I had to keep looking down to check my bearings, worried I might walk into something, or maybe even someone as I stared skyward, but I didn't see the security guard when he approached me.

'Can I help you find something?' he asked.

The sudden voice startled me, making me physically jerk away from him. He was tall and thin and eyeing me cautiously despite my size. His uniform was a jacket, shirt and tie, which were so generic black and white I figured they were most likely supplied by the staff themselves. His name badge, clipped to his left jacket lapel, displayed the name

Austin. 'I don't think so,' I replied, dismissing him, and trying to move on.

He moved instantly to block my progress. 'Normally, visitors uncover their faces when they come inside.'

He didn't like that I had my hoody pulled around to cover most of my face. Annoyed that I had to do this yet again, I reached up with my right hand – my left was pinning the sword in place under my arm – and tugged the hood back just far enough to show him the ruined side of my face.

I got to watch as his haughty, confident expression changed but I didn't get to hear what he might have to say next because a young priest arrived. 'Austin, I believe they need you at the front entrance,' he told the guard quietly. I suspected that was a lie thought up to give the man a reason to move on. Were priests allowed to lie?

The young man looked away while I pulled my hood back into place, then offered me a smile. 'Is there something special you are here for?' he asked. 'A college project, perhaps. I saw you looking at the architecture with great interest. I'm sure you know the cathedral of St Patrick was built in ...'

I decided to go for broke, interrupting him before he could say any more about the building he clearly loved. 'I'm looking for a marker inset in the wall.' I got a surprised look in return, but not a confused one. 'It would be small, perhaps no more than a foot high and most likely ten or more feet in the air. There might be a corresponding marker set into the floor beneath it.'

He shook his head. 'I don't recall ever seeing anything like that,' he said, but something about the way he said it made me challenge him.

'Are priests taught to lie?'

He reacted as he might if I had slapped his face, but like any good punch, the best thing to do is follow it up with another so the opponent has no time to recover.

'The marker leads to an ancient artefact that was most likely moved here when the church was built.' I spoke as if I was an authority on the subject, not someone who only learned about it a few days ago. 'The artefact will be secured inside a box because it cannot be touched without the person doing so dying in a terrible manner.'

The priest was recoiling now, his eyes darting about as he looked for someone to come to his assistance. He was handsome, I noted, a strong jaw that wouldn't look out of place on a billboard or in an aftershave advert, and he was athletic to boot. He was the sort of man I wouldn't mind getting to know if both the world and I were very different. Right now, though, he looked like he were about to shout for help.

'You must have seen footage of the attack in Berlin. Do you know what you were seeing?' I pressed him, stepping close enough that I could smell his cologne. 'The artefact has been hidden here for more than a century and was most likely moved about before that. It possesses untold power if wielded by the right person.'

'And you think you to be that person?' The voice came from behind me as another priest appeared.

'Archbishop,' said the young priest in a relieved manner.

My attention was split between the two of them with one in front and one behind, so I stepped to my right to bring them both into the same shot. 'I mean to find the marker and the artefact. I must ask that you help me with this, but with or without you, I intend to leave here tonight with what I came for.'

The archbishop looked down at me and I had to question what he saw. My jeans and boots were muddy from the fight in hell at Beelzebub's gathering. The coat I wore was far too big and probably made me look like a homeless person and my face was largely hidden inside the hood. I doubted it helped that I look like a child to most people. I was going to try to convince him to help me. But if that didn't work, I was going to do what needed to be done and escape through a portal with Daniel if that was what I had to do.

'What makes you think there is anything here?' he asked, his voice respectfully quiet in the echoey church.

This would be easier if they cooperated, I felt sure of it, and with that in mind, I tried to convince him. 'I already found one of the pieces in England. It was beneath a marker set into the floor in Rochester cathedral. I removed it.'

He snorted a small laugh through his nose. 'I hardly think so, young lady. Had you done so, you would be quite dead. I'm afraid your ignorance betrays you.'

'It was the sword,' I revealed. 'Would you like to see it?' Now I had his attention. Alex had spotted me talking to the two men in their robes and was making her way toward me. 'You were right about it killing anyone who touches it. The verger in the cathedral was foolhardy enough to try it and paid the price.' I slipped my right hand inside DS Spencer's coat which I still used to keep the sword concealed. Plucking the ancient weapon from beneath my left arm to show them, I channelled a small amount of source energy into it at the same time.

The archbishop took a startled pace back, his face registering nothing but shock as he stared slack-jawed at the tiny woman holding the black obsidian sword that glowed with blue light.

I watched his jaw work up and down as he fought for something to say. The glowing weapon was a little too likely to draw attention so I dropped the flow of energy into it and tucked it away again. 'I need the artefact you have here. I need all the artefacts. The end of days is coming, and we have to try to stop it.'

He gawped at me for a moment, but his expression changed from fear to anger in the next heartbeat and he snapped, 'This is blasphemy!' raising his voice so everyone in the building heard him.

I knew it wasn't the place for it, but I swore my disappointment. The archbishop was backing away, turning around so he could signal for help. Dammit, this wasn't what I wanted. I should have waited until they closed and then broken in.

'What's happening?' gasped Alex, arriving at a slow jog.

I didn't feel I needed to explain; the archbishop was making it clear enough. He had the attention of the security guards near the front of the cathedral now and their faces were turned toward me.

The priest grabbed my shoulder. 'This way, quickly,' he begged, already starting down the aisle toward the front of the church. When I didn't move immediately, he said, 'I know where the marker is.'

Chapter 9

I glanced back at the archbishop again. He was near the front entrance now and the security were all moving in his direction, until they saw me start to back away, this is. They saw me make my decision and made one of their own: to stop me. They didn't know what kind of threat I might pose but the archbishop – presumably top of the shop around here – was making plenty of noise and they were ready to do his bidding. If that meant grabbing a girl, then so be it.

I spun around, letting the sword fall free from the coat so I could catch it with my right hand, I went from standing still to full sprint in a heartbeat. Alex hadn't got the message though, so I slammed headfirst into her, my face bouncing off her left boob as I collided with what turned out to be an immoveable object.

I heard an, 'Ooofff!' sound of sharply exhaled air from her as I re-bounded. However, if I had winded her or not, we needed to go. How I managed to keep my footing, I have no idea, but I started running again, yanking at her arm with my free hand.

'Run!' I yelled. She was a big girl, but her stride had to be a yard longer than mine, surely she could keep up. I didn't glance back to find out, I just ran after the priest.

Anton had seen us and was coming our way. His face showed me how confused he was by all that was happening, but I was running after a priest who appeared to be going slow so he wouldn't lose me and behind Alex was a horde of security, their matching jackets making them easy to spot. We ran past worried looking cathedral visitors, their faces just blurs as I tore down the aisle.

As I passed Anton, right on the priest's heels, I yelled, 'Come on!' to make sure he followed and prayed – no pun intended – that the priest was leading me somewhere that wouldn't turn out to be a trap.

A yard ahead of me, his black robes flowing as he ran, he jinked left, vanishing through an archway and down a short corridor.

'Where are we going?' I shouted between breaths that were beginning to get laboured.

The priest slammed into a solid oak door, pulling at his pockets to find a bunch of keys. He too was breathing heavily after running seventy yards. 'The archbishop's private offices,' he managed between gasps, then the key slid into the lock and we were going through the door.

Not a moment too soon though as the security contingent careened around the archway ten yards behind us. Alex was the slowest of us, but she arrived just when the priest opened the door and piled through without slowing down. Her motion almost bowled me over, but the door slammed shut again with us inside. We got half a second of quiet before the security guys hit the other side of it.

'Have they got a key?' I squealed.

'Not with them,' the priest stated confidently. He was crossing the room already, walking now and heading for another large oak door. It looked just like the last door and he was fiddling with the bunch of keys again to find the one he needed. 'They will have to send someone to get it from the master office. We should have at least five minutes.'

The next door opened, the priest sucking in a deep lungful of air as he paused to beckon we follow.

'Did anyone see Spencer?' I asked.

Neither Anton nor Alex had but I couldn't be concerned with that now. The priest had led us into what appeared to be the office of an important person. The room was dominated by a large desk, the type that weighs half a metric ton and is commissioned from a famous master carpenter. The whole room was bedecked with ornate wooden finishes. From the walls to the bookcases to the light fittings, everything looked handmade and worth a fortune.

'Give me a hand,' begged the priest, moving to grab one edge of the huge desk.

'It's beneath the desk?' I asked. This was different from Rochester.

To answer my question in part, he let go the desk to grab a painting behind it. It was a huge oil painting of the last supper and required a fair bit of the priest's ample muscle to lift. As he moved it to one side, though, the symbol appeared. It was etched into the wall and hidden from prying eyes by the painting. We would never have found it without his help.

'Help me put this down, please,' he grunted, straining under the weight. Anton and Alex were closest but only Anton was needed, taking half the load to make it manageable. Then to the desk again which they had to move out of the way to get to the heavy oak sideboard against the wall beneath the marker.

We were working fast, but even so, I could feel the clock ticking and a desperate sense of urgency. If it came to it, I would use sinfire to beat the guards back when they broke through. I needed the artefact and would do whatever it took to secure it now that we were this close.

As we all strained to move the final piece of furniture covering our goal, I had to ask the priest a question. 'Why are you helping me? Haven't you placed yourself in a great deal of trouble?'

'Trouble?' The man paused when he repeated the word. He had his back braced against the wall to give more leverage as he shoved the sideboard away. 'I think I can handle trouble. Aren't you facing something far worse?' I couldn't exactly argue with his point. 'I won't claim to know what is happening in the world, but while I place my faith in God to deliver us all, I also believe he expects us to at least show up to the fight prepared to do some of the work ourselves. I saw you,' he looked directly at me, 'firing balls of light from your hand and I saw you joined by a man who looked just like a rather famous person from my religion.' He was referring to how Godfrey's face, hair, and beard resembled that of the traditional depiction of Jesus. I had mentally labelled Godfrey as Mr Bee Gees to avoid the more obvious connection. 'Whatever is under this floor was hidden here for a reason, but the reason wasn't so it would remain hidden for the rest of all time.'

With a final grunt, the four of us got the sideboard to move another foot and the marker appeared. It was etched into the stone floor just like the last one. How many of these were there? Forty? A hundred? I had no idea how long collecting them might take or how many there might be. However many it was, there was one less to find now.

Alex stared down at the solid-looking piece of stone. 'How do we open it?'

I growled, 'Stand back,' and pushed source energy from my chest into my right arm. My supply of hellfire got depleted back in Rochester, but sinfire should be sufficient to do the job.

We could hear the guards suddenly: they were through the outer door which left just one door between them and us. They slammed into it just as the sparks arcing down my arm reached my hand to form a blue orb of energy. While I focussed on my task, the other three were barricading the door to keep the guards outside. The door opened inward and they were pushing the heavy desk to block it. The guards had greater numbers, but funnelled by the door, they wouldn't all be able to shove at once. I only needed Alex and the guys to buy me a little time.

I lifted my hand, palm extended, then, as Alex grabbed the fascinated priest to pull him back to safety, I drove my hand downward and let the orb go three feet from the ground.

I genuinely wasn't sure what it would do. My experience with source energy could still be measured in days and the only inanimate objects I'd tried it on were a tree and a cell door. It made a mess of them both. In Rochester I got to use a sledgehammer to do this but sinfire did the trick just as efficiently. A blast wave filled with ancient dust blew out from beneath the sideboard as the orb cracked the stone to reveal a gap beneath.

Everyone wanted to look, but I couldn't tell if the armour would be dangerous to them like the sword was so I blocked their view with my back as I got down to the hole to root around with my right hand.

I found what I was looking for instantly, my fingers alighting on a large box. Unlike the one in Rochester, which had been beneath the floor for hundreds of years, this one was still intact. Pulling it from the hole, it was dusty and dirty and had cobwebs and what might be rat poop on it, but otherwise, it looked as good as new. It was two feet long and perhaps ten inches across with a hinged lid.

'They're coming through!' yelled Anton as the door began to open.

The sound of the guards shouting was now in the room, faces appearing around the edge of the door as they began to force their way in. The priest abandoned holding the desk in place to run to a window.

'You can get out here!' he shouted to make sure we all heard.

On the stone floor, I had the box open and the item I found inside in my hand. Daniel had been right: it was a greave; the piece of armour that goes around the shin and calf. It was hardly exciting as pieces of armour go, but I still felt jubilant that we had a piece of the suit because it meant no one else could get it.

An unwelcome voice inside my head said, 'Until they take it from your dead body.' I squashed that thought and ran for the window with the piece of armour in my hand.

The priest was back at the desk, using his strength and weight to hold off the guard for just a few seconds longer. Already on the low window ledge, Anton looked to jump already.

'It's a long way down,' he warned. I couldn't guess how far a long way might be in his head, but we were going to have to go that way regardless.

Looking at the priest for a heartbeat while Alex climbed up to the window, I said, 'Come with us.' It came out like a plea that he save himself from the mire he was about to land in.

I got a wry smile in return. 'This is where I belong. I must face up to what I have done. Go with God, and fight in his name.'

The irony of his statement hit me like an uppercut. I was robbing churches with a plan to kill god when I was done. It wasn't really God, of course, just a being that legend had come to think of as God. The guards shoved the desk another six inches, which shoved the priest forward and into me. In a moment when I let my base instincts take over, I grabbed his head and stole a kiss. For just a second, it reminded me that I might be human.

The moment ended abruptly when the guards shoved the door again. The gap was big enough and they were coming through. With the artefact in my right hand and the sword in my left, I ran, leapt, and sailed out in the black night outside.

Chapter 10

Godfrey

In the peaceful setting of the angels' glamping site, all was far from peaceful. Several arguments had broken out as they disagreed about how to proceed.

The loudest voice was not that of the leader; it rarely was. Godfrey knew that remaining calm when others around him were getting angry, stole their power. And so it was right now as an elder angel raged at him for his choices.

'I told you we needed to pursue your father's armour more than a millennia ago!' the angel shouted. He had silver hair tied into a braid on each side and deeply tanned skin that suggested a life living in a Mediterranean village by the sea.

Godfrey met his shouts with a smile. 'You did, Giannis. However, if you recall, when you raised the subject it was not possible to travel between the realms so it was no more than a hypothesis.'

Giannis wagged a finger at the angels' leader. 'You are avoiding the point, Godfrey. We all know you instructed the humans to hide the armour and the weapons when it became possible to travel to the mortal realm. You could have brought them here. With them we could have defeated Beelzebub.'

The announcement caused murmurs to ripple around the room, clearly not everyone had known it. Godfrey raised a hand. 'It is true that I sent envoys to the mortal realm many hundreds of years ago,' he admitted without shame. 'As soon as the first reports came that it was becoming possible to travel and remain for more than a few seconds, I knew it would be necessary to place the armour out of my brother's reach.' He turned to face Giannis. 'Had I brought my father's weapons and armour here, the demons would have seen it as an act of war and would have come for us.'

'And we would have defeated them,' came a shout from the crowd.

'Ah, Bokerah, thank you,' Godfrey's smile remained intact though there were many voices joining the cry for him to explain why he hadn't taken the step they all felt would have ended the battle with the demons. 'What are we proposing here exactly? Wipe out the demons? I don the armour and challenge my brother openly? He would throw all that he had against us if he believed I had the armour and even if I killed him, there are many powerful demons eager to take his place. Had I worn the armour and challenged them, the last five hundred years would have been filled with senseless fighting, not the peace we have enjoyed.'

'That peace is over now,' pointed out a voice from the crowd. 'The death curse is about to fail.'

'And we need the armour and the sword if we are to win,' argued Giannis again.

Godfrey showed the first sign of irritation when he turned to face Giannis again. Both angels were standing in the centre of a large marquee style tent. It was circular, with the assembly inside lounging on pillows and cushions. Godfrey held centre stage, standing in the middle of the space the cushions surrounded. He turned slowly as he talked, making eye contact with as many people as possible. Rounding on Giannis, he asked. 'How do you propose we obtain them, Giannis? Will you volunteer for the task?'

Giannis had been waiting for the question. It was supposed to be a trap, but he had his retort prepared. 'You refer, of course, to the inconvenient fact that you arranged for the humans to hide the armour on holy ground – the one place in the mortal realm where we cannot easily go.' He was playing up to the crowd now, making what he felt was a winning point. 'Not only that, you entrusted them with hiding it, not only from our enemies, the demons, but also from us, so you have not the slightest idea where they have taken it.'

Godfrey nodded. 'How better to ensure none among us would be so foolish as to attempt to retrieve it when they believed it to be needed.'

'It is needed!' Giannis protested, a large portion of the assembly echoing his thoughts.

'How many times did my father use it?' snapped Godfrey, piercing Giannis so he would know an answer was expected.

Giannis had expected this question too. 'He never needed to, Godfrey. He lived in a different time. There was peace then, a lasting peace. It all ended when your brother killed your father. Or did he?'

Godfrey knew he was losing his audience. His authority, his right to rule had been brought into question before but never more so than in the last week. An anger which he'd held in check for centuries spewed forth now as he whipped around to blast Giannis with both hands. His sustained stream picked up his opponent, sending his body across the room where it barrelled into the crowd, knocking angels flying. Many in the path caught the blast of sinfire energy too, their leader holding his barrage until his mother screamed for him to stop.

His shoulders rising and falling as he panted from the sudden effort and accompanying burst of adrenalin, Godfrey let his arms fall. With hard eyes, he panned around the room. 'The next of you to suggest my brother's claim has any foundation will face me in single combat when the death curse fails.'

His threat silenced everyone. When Beelzebub shouted his claim that it was his brother, Godfrey, and not he who murdered their father, most of the angels were present. It was a full attack, the angels arriving in force to reclaim Gabriel and his son, Samuel, from the demons. Even those who were not there had heard of it since – it was not the sort of thing that a person could keep secret. However, none had been brave enough to question Godfrey directly until now. That he threatened to kill anyone who raised the subject made it likely that none would. It also ensured any who felt it possible Godfrey was his father's murderer would begin to meet in secret if they wished to plot against him.

Now that the assembly were stunned into silence, Godfrey spoke calmly once more. 'There is an issue to which we must attend: The human anomaly Anastasia Aaronson. You all know what she is capable of. Her abilities combined with her humanity will enable her to obtain the armour and I fear she may attempt to do so. The sword is already in play and I know my brother will attempt to seize it from her. My efforts are focussed on preventing that from happening. If I can dissuade Anastasia from tracking down any more parts of my father's armour, I will do so, and I will recruit her to rally behind our cause.' He spun around slowly, taking in all the faces still staring in mute shock after his attack on Giannis. The angel wasn't hurt, of course, merely humiliated. He had been helped back to his feet and stood seething silently at the leading edge of the cushions when Godfrey's gaze reached him.

The leader of the angels let his eyes linger for a moment before concluding. 'I shall leave you to your senseless bickering; if that is what you intend to do. The final battle is coming, and I will be ready. As I assured you, my brother's forces are divided. They will not stand united, and he is most likely throwing everything he has at retrieving the sword.'

Chapter 11

Anton wasn't joking about it being a long drop. It was more than ten feet; too far for me to land on two feet comfortably, especially since I only have one real foot. The stump on my left leg is well healed but jarring the bone would hurt like hell. The darkness outside – we were at the back of the cathedral and in a spot that was not illuminated – also made it hard to judge where the ground was.

I clenched my feet and legs together, braced myself, and when the ground hit, I went with the motion of gravity, rolling down and over as they had taught us for parachute landings in the army. I had only ever done three landings – I wasn't in the paras, so our training had been for interest mostly, and none of them were at night, but what I remembered to do worked, absorbing the impact through the whole of my body, not just the soles of my feet and ankles.

Alex hadn't received such training and was throwing around some choice words as Anton did his best to help her limp away. She looked to be unable to put weight on her left leg. This was not good news when our sole focus ought to be running away.

Above me shouts came from the window and I turned to see a security guard beginning to climb out. I couldn't have them following us now. With a huff of breath, I tucked the greave under my left arm, raised my right hand as I pushed source energy into it and fired a pulse at the bricks just below the window.

It lit the whole area when it struck, blasting loose mortar from the ancient brickwork which fell to the ground amid dying light blue sparks. A single warning shot was enough to give them pause. I imagined they were well-meaning but poorly paid and thus not willing to risk their lives to stop me.

However, I doubted they would give up, not that easily. They would find a different way around and try to intercept us. There were trees to give us cover so they wouldn't see which way we went, and in the darkness I doubted they had seen Alex was limping badly. Whatever the case, I could only count on having bought a small lead and we needed to move.

Running, I caught up with the others.

'She's really hurt her ankle,' wheezed Anton. He was helping her along, but it was extra effort for him, and it slowed us down when we wanted to go fast.

'Daniel can fix it,' I tried to reassure them both. 'He can manipulate source energy to heal. I've seen him do it. We just have to get her to him.'

'It might have to be the other way around,' Alex winced. 'I can't keep going like this and I'm slowing you down. I'm pretty sure I broke it.'

Could we safely leave her and come back? I didn't like that, but perhaps I could go. 'Look, you two tuck in over there.' I pointed to a small brick building. We were at the rear of the cathedral and it looked to be an electrical hub. It would have been erected decades after the cathedral was built when electricity was installed no doubt. 'I'll draw them away and come back for you shortly.'

I think they wanted to argue but there was no point and they knew it. I helped get her a little closer to the low building, but when we heard voices shouting and coming our way, I split off and ran, making myself visible only once I was well away from my friends. Making sure the guards saw me was easy enough, I drew source energy into my core and let a bright glowing orb sit in my right hand as I ran. The greave was beginning to annoy me though. I needed to put it on or something. I needed my right hand to shoot or to hold the sword but two hands to hold the greave and the sword.

I rounded the corner of the cathedral which brought the main street at the front back into sight. There were people visible again a hundred or so yards ahead of me, but I made an abrupt stop once I got around the edge of the building, and popped back out to fire blasts into the ground ahead of the chasing guards. I might even have hit one of them as he ran into my sinfire. It wouldn't do any lasting damage, but it would put him down and that might make his companions go to his aide instead of chasing me. Having bought myself an extra couple of seconds, I thrust the greave toward my right shin. The piece of armour was in two halves: a front and a back connected by a small hinge on one edge. I expected to see a strap with which to connect the two halves on the open side, but there was nothing. Confused, I offered it up to my leg anyway, and watched with astonishment as it melted into my skin.

I reached down to touch my leg and it appeared again. However, where before it had been cool metal, now it was ethereal, a blue glow hovering just outside of my jeans. I tried to touch it, but my hand passed right through. I wanted to ask someone just what the hell was going on, but shouting let me know the guards were still after me.

With a grim smile, I set off running again.

I half expected there to be a second contingent of guards appearing ahead of me. They would not have all abandoned the front entrance to chase us to the archbishop's office, so surely they would be using their radios to liaise and head me off. I ran on anyway, readying myself for a squad to block my path, but as I got halfway down the side of the old building, I could tell there was something happening ahead of me.

Whatever it was, it was causing people to vacate the area. Before I got to the front edge of the cathedral, I could see people running away. There was shouting and screaming and there was the sound of police sirens coming my way. The police sirens were a worry, they had to be coming for me, but taking my next step, the familiar dark red of hellfire exploding lit the street ahead of me and my breath caught in my throat.

The demons had found us again!

Chapter 12

I leapt over a low hedge as I left the grass and met the stone of the cathedral's plaza. It was still well lit by the floodlights and overhead lamps, but now it was all but devoid of people save for those I could see cowering inside the doors as if the building or perhaps the deity it was dedicated to might protect them.

I had no such protection, and a strong need to find Daniel before Beelzebub's forces dragged him away. Losing him would strand me in New York when I needed to be able to travel the planet, but he was also my guide to find more pieces of armour. I also needed him to heal Alex, and he was my back up when I got into a fight.

Ahead of me were steps; a short flight leading down to the street. I wasn't looking at them though, I was staring across to the other side of the road where Daniel was firing orbs of hellfire. He hadn't been taken, which filled me with relief, but only for as long as it took me to track his shots to his attacker.

However, when I found what he was shooting his hellfire at, my mouth dropped open. It wasn't a demon at all, it was a wizard!

At least, my guess was the woman I could see flinging spells his way was a wizard. She was tall, with gorgeous flowing blonde hair that hung over the collar of her winter coat. I took in her appearance before I spotted that she was floating three feet off the ground.

Another fizzing blast of hellfire sped her way, diffusing like the previous ones against a shield of energy she held before her face. The shield had a vague blue glow to it, and symbols I could barely make out etched across its surface. I had seen one just like it last week. Then it was held by a different wizard: Otto Schneider.

I jumped the steps, skidding into the street as a yellow cab screamed by in the road a foot from my toes. The woman whipped her right hand around as above her the air began to crackle and spark. Her hair was standing up like static electricity was pulling at it, and as my hair started to do the same inside my hood, I knew what I was looking at: She was about to release a blast of lightning.

'I've been practicing, Daniel!' she screamed. 'I've been doing nothing but practicing!' She gave a grunt of effort and let the spell go, the air above her head surging forward but anyone trying to track what happened next would have found themselves blinded by the flashes of light that rained down on Daniel.

I screamed for her to stop, torn between running to protect Daniel with my body so that she would hold off her attack, or blasting her myself. However, I knew I was not her enemy. If she is a mortal wizard able to wield elemental magic, then we had to be on the same side. I just needed to make her see that.

There was a car crashed into a traffic light just a few yards from me. I leapt onto the bonnet and called source energy to form sinfire in my right hand. She hadn't seen me yet; her focus was all on Daniel.

The demon had been kicked along the street by the lightning where his trajectory was stopped by a lamppost. From that he bounced painfully back down to the pavement but though smoke rose from his clothes and hair, he was up in a heartbeat and ready to repel her next strike.

'You can practice all you wish, Ayla,' Daniel shouted as he readied two more hellfire orbs. 'Otto can teach you new tricks, but you will never be my equal.'

'Wait!' I screamed as loud as I could.

I think they both heard me, but he sent his hellfire in her direction just as she tore at the ground supporting his feet. She meant to bury him, but I knew it would not be that easy and from what I knew of Otto, his shield had a limited lifespan – hit it enough times and it would fall.

Sooner or later, one of them would lose and I didn't want it to be her. Decision made, I swung my arm around and shot Daniel. My sinfire blast put him through the front of a store window and I finally got Ayla's attention.

'Ayla!' I shouted, lifting my arms out to the sides to show her they were empty. Well, except for the big black sword in my left hand they were empty, but I wasn't holding it in a threatening manner.

Showing shock, she looked my way, but she didn't lower her shield and she didn't drop the spell she held ready in her right hand.

'You're an angel?' she questioned. 'I was told not to trust your race either,' she snarled. The fight had her hopped up and rumbling for more.

'You were told? By Otto Schneider, I assume.' The casual name drop got her attention, her angry grimace faltering for a second. 'I'm not an angel.' I saw her open her mouth to argue, and quickly added, 'I don't know what I am. No one does. I am mortal though and I am asking you to trust me.'

'What's that thing on your leg?' she asked.

I looked down in question, wondering, as I looked if it were a trick. Sure enough, though, the piece of armour I watched dematerialise was back. It coated my leg in a softly glowing translucent blue light.

I looked back up at the woman still holding a spell ready to strike. 'It's armour. I only have one piece so far,' I added to explain why she could only see the piece on my leg.

An angry growl let me know Daniel was up and moving. Without taking my eyes from Ayla, I formed another ball of sinfire and blasted him again. Sirens filled the air. We had seconds before the cops would reach us.

'I don't know who you are or what your beef is with Daniel, but things have changed. He is working with me now against the demons. If you know Otto Schneider, then you know the end of the world is coming. Help me now. Help me to get Daniel and my friends away from this place and I will explain everything. Daniel is not a threat to you anymore.'

Ayla tipped her head back and laughed at my statement. 'I watched him kill innocent people. He has to die, and I will gladly give my life trying to take his.'

The cops arrived; cars screeching to halt to my left and right and there was no more time for words. They were piling out and into the street, taking up defensive positions with their guns ready. I was far from impervious to bullets, and I ran, ducking down behind the debris in the street as I crossed the road and threw myself into the same store I blasted Daniel into.

The cops gave me ample warning before I started running so it was no shock when a hail of bullets came my way. They would think they were dealing with a terrorist attack and act accordingly, shooting first and asking questions if any of the suspects survived. In the world of biological, chemical, and nuclear weapons, and with all the televised strange supernatural events of the last day or so added to it, it was the only safe choice.

I slid across the floor on my belly, keeping low but feeling the sting as shards of glass cut my skin. DS Spencer's trench coat was going to be trash. I needed to get up and find Daniel, but he found me first, grabbing a handful of my hair to yank me off the floor.

'You blasted me with sinfire, Anastasia. That is not part of our deal.' His face was right on mine, his lips close enough to kiss had I wanted to, but he was mad as hell and holding me up by my hair. It hurt enough for me to consider skewering him with the sword.

Through clenched teeth I gasped. 'I have the artefact. We have to go. We can fight later.' I had no idea what might have happened to Ayla, but the cops were coming our way, advancing on foot to close the final yards.

'If I stay here, they will shoot us,' Daniel growled into my face. 'I will survive. Will you?'

I drew source energy into my right hand. 'What do you want, Daniel?'

I thought he was going to lay out a list of demands. But instead, and to my great shock, he kissed me.

Chapter 13

It made my head swim, at least that was what I thought it did, until I realised he had opened a portal and I was falling through it. The kiss broke as my feet touched the grass in the immortal realm. He was no longer gripping my hair either, but that meant I wasn't touching him at all when he opened the next portal and stepped backward through it to vanish.

Staring into the blank space where he had been standing a second before, I could still feel his lips on mine, our breath mingling for the two seconds it lasted. That was how long it took me to wake and see I had been completely suckered and my surprised, yet confused expression was replaced by one of outrage.

'Arrrgh! I'm going to kill him!' I shouted into the darkness. He'd shut me up and shut off my thought processes by something as simple as a kiss. Completely disarmed, he'd taken me to goodness knows where in the immortal realm and ditched me there. He was gone, I had no way of getting back, and now my friends were marooned in New York. He could be there killing them as revenge for me shooting him for all

I knew. I was soooo stupid. I should have kneed him in the nuts the moment his lips touched mine.

Cursing myself, I looked around. There were stars above, but I could have been anywhere on Earth because the landscape was utterly barren. Was the moon laughing at me? Was it? Or could I just hear Daniel's guffaw from the mortal realm where he was probably wandering into a bar with no intention of ever returning for me.

That I had brought this on myself didn't require explaining. I'd been sticking it to Daniel ever since we escaped hell. He was stuck with me; I wasn't wrong about that. Not technically at least. He couldn't return to his home in the countryside and he was probably best served to avoid the immortal realm as much as he possibly could. However, if he truly believed the demons were going to win no matter what, he could easily opt to live out the rest of his days in a drunken state not caring what happened around him. He would have to keep moving to stay ahead of the sun but that wasn't taxing for him and he would be immortal until the death curse fell.

No one knew when that would be.

One thing was for certain: I was in trouble. Squinting into the darkness and turning a slow circle, I confirmed there was no good direction in which I could head. I would have to wait until morning and pray the sunlight revealed something the moon could not.

The familiar dull pop of a portal opening spun me around to face a welcome pool of shimmering air. It was Daniel, and he had Alex, Anton, and DS Spencer with him.

'Sorry that took so long,' he apologised. 'I paused a moment to heal her foot first.'

'It feels as good as new,' boasted Alex, stamping it on the ground experimentally.

A moment ago, in the store in New York, he had lifted me from the floor by my hair. Then he kissed me. Now he was acting like neither thing had happened. It was making my head spin. I'm only twenty-three, I shouldn't have to face all these conflicting emotions and problems. It was bad enough trying to fight my hormones, without badass hot demons triggering them while I'm doing my best to focus on saving humanity from slavery or extinction.

'Where to next, boss?' he asked me.

His casual ... nay, obedient attitude was making my right eye want to twitch. I had no idea where to go next, I wanted to ask him a whole bundle of questions, including the one about why he chose to kiss me in a manner intended to make me remember the kiss, but I put it all aside to deal with the question first in line.

'Who's Ayla?'

He blew out a frustrated breath and kicked a loose rock across the ground. 'A former familiar.'

'Someone you kidnapped and enslaved,' I translated.

'What?' asked DS Spencer. 'You kidnap and enslave people?'

I could see the conversation going downhill fast if I didn't steer it. 'Daniel made a living enslaving humans who demonstrated magical ability. They became slaves to demons, though they call them familiars. He would find them, snatch them from Earth, and take them to the immortal realm from where they could not escape. There, he would train them until they were of a useable standard. Is that about right?' I asked him to confirm.

'You make it sound seedy?' he complained.

DS Spencer shook his head. 'It's criminal.'

'Only on Earth,' Daniel argued, his haughtiness returning. 'Humans were *familiars*,' he said the word loud to remind me that in his language it meant something different to slave, 'to my race long before they learned to count or write or even think. Humans are worse. You made slaves of your own race.'

He had a point.

I steered the conversation back on track. 'Anyway, who is Ayla? She seemed upset with you.'

With an angry grimace Daniel told me, 'She is one of Otto Schneider's. He freed hundreds of familiars a short while ago. It ruined me, taking my standing down enough pegs that my worth began to be questioned. I did my best to turn that around, recapturing or, ... killing,' he mumbled, 'those escapees I could find and recruiting more to replace those who had been lost. Ayla was one who escaped. She is a New York native and was also the first familiar I forced Otto to steal.'

'How did she find you tonight?' I wanted to know.

He shrugged. 'Pure chance. In a city that size, we could walk past each other a dozen times, passing within feet of each other and never notice. Tonight, she spotted me and … well, you saw what happened.'

'Take me to her,' I insisted.

Now he swung his eyes to look at me. 'What?'

'I need to locate the other artefacts. How many other locations are you sure of?'

'Sure of?' he echoed. 'Maybe two. They were hidden by men on the instruction of Godfrey and this was hundreds of years ago. Many have been moved since, but they were distributed between the various religions, each creating their own secret sect to hide and protect the artefact they were entrusted with. I found out about the one in New York when I stumbled across an old archbishop's diary. I say stumbled but, of course, I was researching with a view to finding the sword. That would have been the final piece in my ascension. Presenting that to Beelzebub at the right time would have cemented my position at his side.'

I clicked my fingers to stop the stupid demon from reminiscing. 'Hey, Daniel. It's over, Beelzebub wants to eat your liver for breakfast. You're a big disappointment, remember.'

He let out a forlorn sigh before continuing. 'There is almost certainly one in Barcelona, and I think there is one in London. Other than that, I just cannot be sure where they might be. I don't think any went to Australia or Africa, when the armour was distributed, they weren't developed enough to be included. Neither was America for that matter but, like I said, many have been moved over the years as better hiding places came up.'

I nodded at Alex. 'Okay, so that's two out of forty or more that we still need to find. I need you to do the research, but I can't take you home because the police will be watching for you.'

'Or the goons from the SIA,' DS Spencer reminded us.

'I can't go to work either for the same reason,' Alex concluded.

'That's right. If I can convince Ayla to help, we can get you into a library near her – New York must have a good one. Do you think you can find what we are looking for?'

Alex puffed out her cheeks. I was asking a lot: You can't go home. You're a wanted person now because I knocked on your door and it's probably going to get worse. Don't worry about that though, just help me find some ancient artefacts hidden where no one should ever accidentally find them and if there are any clues to their whereabouts, they too are most likely hidden behind centuries of secrets and lies.

'I can try,' she agreed.

I would thank her properly later. Right now, we were hanging around in the dark in the immortal realm and it wasn't a clever place to be. 'You know where Ayla lives?' I asked Daniel.

Chapter 14

DS Spencer volunteered to be the one who would knock on her door. We were in a pleasant suburb of New York. There were driveways and front lawns, two-car garages, and trees clinging to the last few leaves as Autumn hit the area hard.

The rest of us weren't out of sight, but we were respectfully back from the property, standing on the pavement that ran alongside the road. I made sure I was in clear sight and asked Ralph to stand to one side after he knocked on the door so it was clear we were not trying to hide anything.

I didn't have to worry about Ayla instantly going into attack mode because she didn't answer the door. A man, presumably her husband, did.

'Good evening,' said the British detective in an accent that immediately made the man inside the house raise his eyebrows. 'I was hoping to speak with Ayla.' He showed the man his police identification. 'You may be questioning what business a detective from England could possibly have with the lady of the house.'

The man spoke for the first time. 'I sure am. I'm a New York cop. Is this to do with what happened earlier today?' he asked. 'Ayla said there was a girl there with an English accent.'

'That was me,' I waved to him from the street. 'I'm not a girl. Actually, I'm a former soldier. I'm just small. Can we talk to her? I need her help. It's about when she went missing.' I hazarded a guess that the woman would have been missing for a period when Daniel snatched her but hadn't thought to ask him about it until now. Too late to confirm it wasn't a few hours and the husband might never have noticed, I had guessed right, because he jutted his head out to check if his neighbours were listening, then beckoned for all five of us to get inside quickly. He didn't want people to know.

Self-conscious as always when I meet new people, I tugged my hood forward a little to hide the scar and moved some of my hair around to cover it. Next to me, Daniel cricked his neck to one side and then the other before rolling his shoulders as if limbering up for a fight.

'We need her,' I reminded him. 'If she tries to kill you, go with it, don't start flinging hellfire around. You are the one in the wrong.'

'Only from your perspective,' he argued. 'Anyway, since you are being all big picture and wanting to recruit people, you might want to consider hiding less. That scar isn't as offensive as you think it is.'

He stepped over the threshold and into the house of a person he once came here to kidnap but left me standing on the driveway outside as I tried to decipher his comment. What the heck did he mean, it isn't offensive? Is he saying *he* doesn't find it offensive? Does that mean he doesn't think I'm ugly?

'You coming in?' asked the husband, holding the door still but clearly wanting to close it before all the heat in his house escaped.

The sound of crockery smashing somewhere deep in the house got my feet moving. The husband's too as his wife shrieked. The door got left open – it wasn't mine to shut and it never occurred to me – as we both ran through the house. I expected to see a doorway ahead of me filling with flashes of bright light and prayed none of it would be dark red, but when I crashed through the door to what proved to be their kitchen, hot on the heels of Ayla's husband, I found Daniel backed into a corner with Alex, Anton, and DS Spencer forming a human shield to protect him.

Ayla was snarling with anger yet again, her teeth bared and her hair floating as she held a spell ready to deploy.

'Please,' I begged her. 'If we have any hope of stopping Armageddon, we have to work together.'

Her eyes were locked on Daniel, daring him to move and I worried she would kill my friends if he did. 'Work together? With a demon?' she spat the word.

From the corner of the room behind her, a small voice cried out, 'Mommy!' I hadn't seen her children cowering behind the dining table. They were terrified, but I wasn't sure who they needed to be more scared of.

'No harm is being threatened, Ayla,' I pointed out putting my own body between her and everyone else. 'I get why you don't trust Daniel. But you need to trust me.' Her gaze remained firmly locked on her target until I raised the glowing sword and added, 'Because I can kill him.'

Finally holding her attention, I pulled back my hood; something about what Daniel said scored a hit. If I constantly hid my face, would people trust me? The sword illuminating my face with a soft blue glow must have highlighted my scar because she stared at it with her mouth open and she finally softened.

Ten minutes later the tension in the room was still high but no one was trying to kill anyone else. 'Uncle' Detective Sergeant Ralph was doing magic tricks for the kids with Anton and Ayla's husband in a room they called 'the den' and us girls were having a hard talk while Daniel listened quietly from the corner.

Ayla had a large glass of wine on the go when we arrived. She said she arrived home still shaking with adrenalin and shock. I believed her and was grateful when she extended the invitation of a glass to Alex and me.

I really wanted a beer, but it would be impolite to ask for what was not offered. 'You killed a demon,' Ayla repeated. 'I thought they were immortal.'

'We are,' said Daniel. Ayla had banned him from speaking, her concession when I begged she let him stay in the house. She shot him a hard look, to which he mimed zipping his mouth closed, locking it, and throwing away the key.

I let go a shuddering breath and sank into a dining chair. 'Apparently, Nathaniel was the first to die in over four thousand years. The first since the death curse trapped them all in an alternate reality.'

'But you said you killed more since?' she tried to confirm.

'That was yesterday,' I started to say, then had to stop to correct myself. 'Hold on, no, I guess technically, it was today even if it is tomorrow in England now.'

Alex put her hand on my arm. 'When did you last sleep, Ana?'

I shrugged. 'I don't know. In the police cell maybe. That would be three days ago or something now. I've totally lost track with the shifting between realms and crossing time zones.'

'You look ruined,' she said. Alex wasn't being unkind, but I wanted to bristle against her comment anyway. It was one thing I learned early on in the army: sometimes you just don't get a chance to sleep. You keep going until the fighting stops and then you rest. Before I could speak again, Alex started explaining things to Ayla. 'There are more of the pieces of armour we talked about. I need access to the internet, and ideally, I need to get to a library with a decent research centre. Can you help us with that?'

'Because the British police think you are all terrorists and will lock you up if you attempt to go home?' she confirmed.

Alex made a glum face. 'That's about the size of it, yes.'

Ayla snorted a sad laugh. 'If I didn't know what I know, I would kick you out and call the police. Or I would summon the elements and do what I could to kill you all. Otto convinced me there is hope though, so I will help you while I reach out and try to find him.'

'How long has it been since you saw him?' I asked.

She had put her wine glass down and was about to move away when my question made her pause. 'I haven't seen him since the night he returned me here. He rescued hundreds of familiars, bringing us back to Earth through a portal he conjured even though no mortal has ever been able to cross between the realms of their own accord. Something went wrong though,' her hard eyes returned as she looked at Daniel once more. 'Something Daniel did interrupted the portal and it scattered the familiars. There was a facility in Bremen waiting for us. They had medical aid and people on hand to help because some of the people had been trapped in the immortal realm for hundreds of years. They would need to be slowly reintroduced to the world.' She paused to lock eyes with each of us. 'Imagine seeing a car or a plane for the first time. We don't know where they went, but they didn't stay in the immortal realm and they didn't arrive in Bremen. So far as I know, he has been trying to find them ever since.'

Daniel had the good sense to stay quiet. It was probably an admission of guilt and I already knew he had been tracking down and killing the escaped familiars, but I didn't think it wise to let Ayla know.

She left the room, and I guess I let my eyes close for a moment because when I woke up the house was silent.

'You're awake,' said Daniel from somewhere in the darkness. His voice made me twitch and twitching made me realise I didn't have the sword in either hand. Given its deadly nature and the fact that it could mean victory or defeat for humanity, I had been somewhat reluctant to let it go. And that was why I now jumped up in panic. 'I have it,' Daniel let me know, guessing that it was the absent sword that had me flustered.

'Why do you have it?' I asked, trying to keep the accusation from my voice.

He got to his feet, making himself visible as moonlight coming through the window outside caught the side of his face. 'The kids wanted to see it. I doubted you would be pleased if one of the humans touched it out of curiosity.' The mental picture of a child sharing the same fate as the verger in Rochester was abhorrent.

He held something aloft that was clearly not the sword. It looked like a long thin, canvas bag. 'Clint found a shotgun bag for you to keep it in,' he explained as he handed it over.

A bag. Genius. It was completely encased and safe from accidental touching by anyone. The bag also had a shoulder strap so I could keep my hands free. I took the bag and looped it over my head. The sword fell against my back where it hung comfortably. This was much better.

'Where is everyone else? No, hold on, what time it is? How long have I been asleep?'

Daniel waited for the barrage of questions to cease, then answered each in turn. 'Everyone is asleep accept Ayla and Alex, they are next door using computers to research our particular problem. Ayla refused to entertain going to bed with me in her house. I guess I shouldn't find that surprising. It is close to four in the morning and you have managed about seven hours sleep. I thought about moving you a few times but worried I might wake you. I hope you are not stiff from being on the chair for so long.'

What was this? It sounded like genuine concern from the demon. First a kiss, then a faint sign of attraction, now concern. It might have been innocent enough, but it was making me feel wary. I wasn't dumb enough to trust him, even though I desperately wanted to.

The sound of light footsteps in stockinged feet heralded the arrival of my host. Ayla came through the door eyeing Daniel warily still. Alex was right behind her.

My librarian friend gave me a smile. 'I want to say you look better after some sleep, but you honestly don't.'

'Thank you, Alex' I laughed. 'That's so good to hear.'

Ayla interrupted. 'You must want a shower. I called a friend who has a kid about your size.' She shot me an apologetic look. 'I figured you would want some clean clothes.'

She wasn't wrong. I followed her eyes down to my hoody and jeans. My clothes were battered and muddy and torn in places. There were even stains which were probably my blood. I knew I needed to set off on my quest again as soon as possible. Quest: what a crazy word to use, but I could think of none better. My life had gone down the toilet. I was wanted by the police and my flatmate was dead. The world thought I might be a terrorist which meant I had nowhere to live and if I didn't have Daniel around to remind me that it was all real, I might just assume I was mental.

I looked back up at Ayla. 'A shower sounds amazing, thank you.'

She backed out of the door saying, 'I sent Clint to buy disposable toothbrushes and fresh underwear. I guess the panties won't be your style, and I wouldn't have sent my husband, but I wasn't prepared to leave the house with the demon and my family in it.' Daniel was wise enough to say nothing.

Ayla led me to the foot of the stairs and started heading up. Back in the kitchen, Alex was telling Daniel what she had already found. I was trying to listen to two different people and got about half of what each was saying. Ayla was mostly apologising for the hoody she had for me and because I was only half listening, I didn't get why until I saw it.

I had to save the world wearing a My Little Pony motif across my chest. Worse yet, the hoody had a tail at the back. I know beggars can't be choosers, but it felt like fate was already giving me the finger today and the sun wasn't even up. Thinking about the sunrise propelled me onwards and into the shower. Daniel needed to move before the sun appeared on the horizon. In late November we had at least a couple of hours, but he would be getting twitchy soon.

Using the tall mirror in the family bathroom, I stripped, and while the shower was getting up to temperature, I inspected my body. The bruises and cuts I expected to find, and was wondering why I couldn't feel, were strangely absent. Daniel had healed me while I was sleeping. That was the only explanation I could come up with. Unless immortality was catching, which sounded less likely. It was another question to itch away at the back of my head – why had he done it? Daniel made it clear his world and all his actions were for the benefit of himself. Something as selfless as healing me because he could was out of character. I wanted to believe he could and possibly had changed, but it felt more likely he was doing these things because of a selfish motivation I could not yet perceive.

My biggest problem, I acknowledged as I stepped under the hot water, was how unfairly good looking he was and how attracted I was to him.

Mercifully, one might argue, showering and cleaning myself is such a chore with a missing hand and a missing foot, that I soon forgot all about Daniel's muscular body and chiselled jaw. I almost fell over twice, but worried I might wake those who were asleep, I got the job done quietly and dressed myself again.

The bathroom was so full of steam, getting the new clothes on was a task; a person would choose to go elsewhere to cool down first, but in someone else's house that wasn't an option for me.

Bereft of makeup, my hair still damp, but clean and feeling ready for the day, I made my way back downstairs to find Daniel and Alex talking. Ayla was making coffee, the strong scent reaching my nose to lure me in.

Alex put an arm around my shoulders to pull me into a hug as I got close. 'How are you feeling?' she asked.

'A lot more human than I did.' Ayla turned at the sound of my voice, raising her eyebrows in question as she held up the coffee pot. I nodded. 'Yes, thank you. Thank you for the clothes too.'

Ayla grimaced as she looked at me. I looked like a scarred thirteen-year-old girl. 'I haven't been able to reach Otto yet,' she let me know.

Alex tracked Ayla's eyes, only then taking in my hoody. 'Oh, goodness,' she chuckled.

'Yeah, yeah, big joke,' I sighed. 'She's got a magical hand cannon and she's wearing a My Little Pony top and day-of-the-week knickers.'

'Are you?' asked Daniel sounding distinctly interested and ogling my butt.

I turned to face him, but it didn't seem to make much difference to the direction his eyes were aimed. I said, 'Hey!' to get his attention, and when his were looking at mine again, I asked, 'Aren't you supposed to want to get going?'

'Pretty soon,' he agreed. 'We have a destination. I was merely waiting for you.'

I sipped at my coffee, feeling it working a different kind of magic as it charged my veins with caffeine. 'Where are we going?' I asked.

'I think I might have found something at a temple in Osaka,' Alex announced. A yawn split her face. 'It's really fascinating stuff, trying to track down where unlisted artefacts the world doesn't know exist might be hidden.'

I frowned deeply. 'How exactly are you doing it then?'

She yawned again and pointed an arm at Daniel and her face split to force her eyes closed. When she finally beat the yawn into submission, she said, 'He tipped me off.'

Daniel raised his right eyebrow. 'I did?'

'You said you tracked the sword by finding extracts from diaries,' she explained. 'Well, the further you go back in time, the rarer such things become. We can only use the internet because of the time of day here but it is filled with information,' she told us, her voice brimming with enthusiasm. 'By using a cipher to cross reference data points,' she yawned again and we had to wait for it to finish, 'we were able to find numerous instances where words like hide, conceal, or bury were used in conjunction with the names of synagogues, cathedrals or other religious buildings. It appears to be limited to very old places of worship.'

'So, what's in Japan?' I had to ask.

She scratched her head. 'I'm not entirely sure.'

It wasn't the answer I was hoping for, but it was an answer and better than I could have done by myself, especially since I had been asleep while Alex was working. Turning to Daniel, I said, 'Ready?'

Chapter 15

Before we left Ayla's house, Alex explained that she had found other targets that looked likely, including something in Egypt that she believed might be a motherload. I didn't hang around to hear the full explanation, but she was onto something and I had to hope she had it right. We couldn't go to Egypt: travelling with the sun meant going west from where we were.

As long as Daniel stayed in the dark, we could be anywhere, but apparently you couldn't fool the system by hiding Daniel underground. If he were in a part of the world on which the sun shone, it would reject him.

From Ayla's house in New York, he bounced us into the immortal realm and out again faster than I could draw a breath, landing us in a quiet back alley that smelled of fish. I knew nothing of Osaka, but one lungful of local air was all I needed to determine that it was by the sea. I could practically taste the salt in the air.

'What time is it here?' I asked.

'The time difference is thirteen hours. That's why we waited so long in New York. If we left earlier, we would have arrived while it was still light and were it not so late in the year, the sun would still be up here. It set fifteen minutes ago.'

That still didn't tell me what time it was, but I guessed it had to be late afternoon if the sun had only just gone down. I had already established that Daniel didn't know anything about the temple we were going to raid. Nor did he know where it was from where we were, but leaving the alleyway to emerge onto a busy street, I got my first taste of Japan.

I couldn't say why, but my eyes expected a scene from the past. We were in a fishing village on the coast and there ought to be old people wearing hats and simple frocks as they carried buckets of fish about. Instead, my eyes were assailed by the same things I see back home. Young people wearing designer labels, neon lights, and flashy new cars.

While I was busy taking all that in, Daniel had orientated himself. He'd been to Japan before, and I want to say that he admitted it was in the pursuit of familiars but the way he said it wasn't an admission, it came out more like he was bragging. He felt no shame over the way he had treated humans and I doubted he ever would.

The name of the temple was Shitennoji which, of course, made me giggle childishly. 'Shit an oji? What's an oji?' I chuckled, entertaining myself and genuinely surprised I was still capable of finding things funny.

Daniel merely pointed his hand in the direction we needed to go, defusing my mirth by ignoring it. Once I could see it, he stopped walking.

He didn't say anything though, so with my eyes on the incredible sight of the ancient temple, I only knew he wasn't next to me when his raised voice called out from ten yards behind me, 'Good luck.'

I turned around to find him two yards behind me. 'Good luck?' I echoed. 'That's all I get.'

I got a curious look from him in return. 'What? You want a hug? You're the chosen one, Anastasia. I'm just a demon. I couldn't even go with you if I wanted to.'

'The chosen one?' Now I was just repeating his words. 'Why did you kiss me?' The sudden change of conversation hadn't been planned. I was feeling pissy toward him and the words just happened to find their way out of my mouth.

I got a wolf's grin and a wry snort of laughter. 'You were annoying me,' he chuckled. 'It was kiss you or punch you in the mouth. I figure it's probably been a while since you were kissed.' He was laughing at me and it made me want to blast him with sinfire.

My messed-up memory meant I couldn't remember ever being kissed. At the edge of my brain there were tantalising images, half-glimpsed memories of past encounters, of boyfriends or one-night stands. I couldn't tell which they were but knowing I must have kissed in the past didn't change the fact that the kiss he stole was effectively my first and he was making me feel bad about it. It cleared up one thing though: he wasn't into me at all, he was that same total dick he'd been since I met him.

Through clenched teeth, I hissed. 'Please be here when I get back.' He was probably grinning as I walked away, so I didn't check to look, knowing that to do so would give him even more satisfaction. Trying to focus my mind on the task of finding the marker somewhere inside the temple, I pulled a little source energy into my core. The power aided my confidence. If I chose to, I could send the energy down my right arm and into my hand where it would instantly become an effective weapon, but not one that would kill a human if I hit them with it. This time when I did it, I felt the greave on my right shin like it flashed into life briefly to remind me it was there. There was something else though, something tugging at me. It was gone by the time I could identify that it wasn't my imagination.

The sword was across my back still inside the shotgun bag where it would stay until I needed it. You might wish to argue that if I needed it, the process of getting it out would take altogether too long, and you would be right, but walking around with a shiny black three-foot blade tends to get too much attention.

Access to the gardens around the temple was free. I passed through a gate and into a beautiful setting that would be perfect to share with a special someone; a stray thought which was confirmed by the number of couples I could see walking arm in arm along the winding paths. I passed around them, but looking for a way to get into the temple, which had closed for the day, another series of thoughts occurred to me: I discovered my ability to channel source energy just a few days ago. I did some mental arithmetic and came up with twelve days. The changing time zones was messing with my head, but it was something like that. I'd taken myself into the woods to practice flinging sinfire and to see what else I could do a couple of times, but I knew there were other things I ought to be able to do. Daniel could manipulate source energy to heal people, he could create a thin whip which he then used to torture me. Okay, I wasn't exactly desperate to learn that one, but there had to be so many other tricks I could discover. Otto Schneider could fly. He used elemental magic for that but was it something I could do? I didn't know the answer, but I knew I needed to find time to explore my abilities.

Back to the task at hand, I looked around. Having moved around the garden, I'd been able to find an empty spot. I needed to cross an ornate stream which I leapt easily since it was only a yard across at the narrow point I found. I slipped through the bushes on the other side, vanishing from sight before the next visitors came into sight. The temple was surrounded by an outer wall which was just as ornate as the rest of it.

Were there cameras aimed at the wall and being monitored in a security shack somewhere? Probably was the only answer I could come up with. I would have to be fast then, if such a thing were within my power. Pulling in source energy for confidence again, I started to scale the wall, but stopped instantly when I felt the odd tugging sensation again. It happened the moment I drew in source energy. Despite believing the longer I hung around by the wall, the more likely I was to get spotted, I stepped down to the ground again. There, I dropped the source energy I held and drew in a fresh charge. This time I was feeling for the tug and I got a jolt of excitement when I realised it was coming through the greave.

Don't ask me how I knew, or why I was confident in my belief, but I felt utterly certain the armour was calling to the other piece. It was in the temple somewhere but unlike New York, this time I could feel a direction.

Energised, I went over the wall, and moving fast, I followed the sensation. Constantly dropping and reconnecting my link to the source energy was like using a homing beacon. However, as I hurried on through the deserted grounds of the temple, like breaking out of jail or a prisoner of war camp, I was waiting for a searchlight to suddenly illuminate me and the shouts of guards to come my way.

I could feel my heart banging in my chest, but I continued onward without challenge, getting closer, I hoped, to the target. That I believed the artefact hidden here was calling me to it now was a cheering thought. I would have to search the temple, but as I snuck inside the building, I saw that things were not going to be as easy as I might have hoped.

The temple was filled with Buddhists at prayer. I didn't know much about Buddhism, but I was fairly certain they would disapprove of me disturbing them to steal something hidden inside the oldest temple in the country.

Hiding in the shadows by the door, I huffed out a breath and considered my options. I was here and I was going to get the artefact. One option was just to accept the task and do whatever was necessary to get the job done. I wouldn't have to hurt anyone, but if they tried to stop me, it was probable that I would have to fling some sinfire around. I dropped my link to the source and re-energised it, letting the tugging sensation draw me to the left.

As quietly as I could, I crept across the open entrance of the temple and slunk along the dark outer edge of the large room. There had to be over a hundred men at prayer, I didn't think any of them were women, and they were all in neat lines as if set out on a grid.

No one looked my way as I slipped from the room and into another, much smaller, chamber. Really, it was a room with windows on two sides and a corridor leading out of it from the opposite side to the one I had just entered through. I made my way to the corridor, but as I did so, the feeling of being drawn forward changed. It made me stop moving and look down. The marker, the same one as I found before in both Rochester and New York, was in the floor. I looked up to find it also carved into the ceiling. The ceiling was wooden, but the floor was a stone tile and it extended to the walls on both sides. I swore under my breath and looked about fruitlessly for a way to get under the tile without smashing it. I don't know why I bothered; the floor of the temple had been there for fifteen hundred years. So long in fact that foot traffic over the marker had worn it almost smooth.

Seeing no alternative, I pushed power into my right arm and got ready to blast the floor apart. Hold on though. The temple was so old, the floor had to have been laid before the angels could return to Earth to collect the armour. How then was it under the floor? The answer was that it had to have been placed there afterwards and that meant there had to be a way to lift the stone.

I was going to work out how and then carefully extract the artefact without disturbing the peace.

A cry of alarm changed my mind.

Startled by the shout, which broke what had until then felt like an impenetrable silence, I jumped and accidentally loosed the orb of sinfire in my hand. It shot across the chamber and blew a hole in the wall.

Staring at the moonlight coming in through the freshly made window, I swore loudly with embarrassment. The temple had stood all this time, undoubtedly weathering storms and earthquake, fires and flood, and maybe even marauding invaders, but could it survive Anastasia Aaronson?

The shout that startled me came from an old man who appeared to have stumbled across me as he made his way from somewhere to somewhere else. He recognised me for what I was: a thief. Come to take what was not mine, his shouts were echoed by more voices as others came to his aid.

I had no time, a big language barrier to overcome, and a sudden need to pee which could not be satisfied where I was. With a grunt of effort, I drew in more source energy, darted back a step, and flung it all into a sustained stream that melted clean through the ancient stone floor.

The old man shielded his face from the bright light but continued to shout his displeasure. Gasping for breath and feeling a little spent, I ran to the hole and peered inside. Unfortunately, the blast of sinfire had created a storm of dust as it went through the stone and seeing anything in the hole was impossible.

Falling to my knees, I shoved my right hand into the blackness beneath floor level and did my best to root around. I found nothing, not even a spider's web. Just how deep was the hole? With more source energy called to firm an orb in my hand, I tried to illuminate the space, but I was out of time and the angry congregation of Buddhists were coming for me. Not that I blamed them for wanting to stop me, I still couldn't allow it.

They were all rushing me from the same direction as the old man who was still yelling in Japanese. I could run away along the corridor that led out of the chamber, or I could blast a fresh hole in a wall and get out that way, but I wasn't leaving without the piece of armour so I did neither thing.

Instead, I stood my ground.

A newly formed sinfire orb got their attention, especially when I fired it into the floor by the advancing crowd's feet. This time, I didn't put much into it and it merely made the stone glow for a moment as the energy dissipated out.

'Anyone speak English?' I asked, hopefully.

They had entered the room and fanned to fill the space before me. They didn't look friendly, but equally, they were not acting overtly aggressive.

A rough voice replied to my question. 'I speak English. Who are you?' I connected a face to the voice as he pushed his way through the press of men to reach the front row.

I pushed back my hood to reveal my face and hoped they would see that I wasn't a child in from the street. 'My name is unimportant,' I told him. 'I am here to collect an ancient piece of armour buried beneath your temple. I apologise for the mess, but the magnitude of my task will not allow for discussion.' I was trying to speak as plainly as I could, but probably not doing a very good job.

As he did his best to translate, I held them at bay with another blue orb and continued to glance into the hole. How deep was it? Did I jump and trust that it was only a couple of feet deep? What if there were spikes at the bottom? What if it was an old well they had covered over? How would I get out?

Now, I don't want to use the word wizened in case it sounds derogatory, but the crowd parted to let an old man through and if I had to guess his age, it would be about a hundred and fifty. He used a short walking stick, short because he was several inches shorter than me which made him small for a human, let alone short for a man, but whatever his title, he held status in the temple because all trace of murmuring going around the room ceased as he became visible.

I swallowed hard under his gaze, not that I could see his eyes, his face was so wrinkly and scrunched up. Despite the orb in my hand that was keeping his brethren at bay, the old man continued to wobble forward, closing the distance until he was less than three feet from me at which point he stopped and looked up.

For a start, I wasn't used to having people look up at me. Children do, but I don't know anyone with children and even if I did, they end up taller than me by the time they reach puberty. His stature didn't unnerve me though, his steady gaze did. However, it was when he spoke that he really caught me off guard.

'I have been expecting you,' he revealed in perfect English. His accent had a trace of Oxford about it, suggesting he had learned my language outside of Japan. 'You are here for what my ancestors buried, yes?'

I managed to say, 'Um.' My mouth had gone dry, and my tongue felt too big, but I managed to nod my head to answer his question. How could he be expecting me?

Without taking his eyes from me, he spoke over his shoulder in his native tongue, the instant result of which was half a dozen men darting forward.

I tensed instantly, more energy surging into the sinfire I still held ready to fling, but the old man said, 'There is no need for concern. We were only ever the keepers of the artefacts. We could never use them. Our role was to watch over them until the time came for them to be employed once more. I see that destiny has chosen well. You have endured much and survived to become stronger than you know.'

I felt like I should curtsey or say thank you, but I took a step back as the men approached the hole I made.

Watching them, I could not help but ask the question, 'How do you know what I am? How do you know I am the right one to collect the artefacts?' Upon asking the question it occurred to me he used the plural not the singular: artefacts, and a beat of excitement passed through me that there might be multiple items hidden here.

To my great surprise – honestly, this was one of those blow-me-down-with-a-feather moments – the old man lifted his right hand and conjured flame into it. 'My abilities have weakened in my latter years, but I am attuned enough to know that whoever came for it would possess a power vastly different from mine. Long have I pondered the true nature of our world and the mysteries within it. You can harness the same power as the devas,' I assumed by devas he meant angels, 'I do not know what they are, only that they defy the laws of man and have never been able to enter this temple, nor any other temple that I know of. That you can, and your refusal to use your power against us when it would have made your egress with the artefacts simpler, tells me you are the one who we have been safekeeping this for.'

Three men had carefully lowered a fourth into the hole where he vanished completely from sight to demonstrate how deep it was. Grunting and straining from the darkness beneath concluded with a large wooden box appearing. The man in the hole pressed it over his head, getting it high enough for the men on the surface to lean in and take it.

I could barely suppress my excitement when they slid it over the stone floor. It was sealed, and though dirty, it was still in good condition. The box was almost three feet square and a foot and a half deep. It could be filled with pieces. One might argue they are all important but there is a reason soldiers wear an armour plate on their chest not on their hip.

Tools appeared, fetched at the old man's command, the box coming open moments later with a screeching noise from some of the nails and a popping noise from others as they simply gave up. I don't know how long I took between breaths when the lid came off, the pessimistic part of me laughing that there would be a single piece of insignificant armour sitting in the middle like a giant birthday present with a tiny toy inside.

That wasn't the case. I knew instantly what I was looking at because I'd borrowed Alex's phone to look up pieces of armour. I was looking at the placard which went right around the chest and back to protect them, and the guard brace that went over the shoulders and upper arms.

Before I could stop him, the nearest man reached in with his hands to pick it up.

I screamed, 'No!' in terror but unlike when the verger touched the sword, the man didn't writhe and contort in a death spasm of agony. He just looked shocked, as did everyone, as my shout echoed. I put my hand to my chest but didn't explain my fear for he was already getting to his feet with the armour in his hands. It came as a single piece which he offered to lift over my head.

Suddenly conscious I still held sinfire in my hand, I drew it back into my body and took off the sword. Placing the long green canvass bag on the ground, I ducked slightly to pop up inside the armour. Like before with the greave, it seemed somehow to shrink to fit my dimensions and then vanished, sinking through my clothes to become a part of me. Awed mutterings rose from the spectators watching me, and the old man said. 'Truly, it was intended for you.'

Was it? How could that be true? He made it sound as if there were an ancient prophecy about one who would come to save the world, but that wasn't me. I was just a petite girl from England. I was missing bits and devoid of memory, but what did that tell me? What would I know if my memory was intact?

I didn't get time to consider the question because my onlookers were waiting for me to do something. It was probably time for me to leave, but as I marvelled at how easy this had been, an explosion ripped through the air and through the fresh hole I made in the wall of the ancient temple, I got to watch a fireball leap into the air.

Oh, crap!

Chapter 16

I didn't bother to thank anyone or say goodbye, I swooped my right arm down to grab the shotgun bag and ran. I didn't go for the corridors leading from either end of the room though, I made a beeline for the fireball, and at the wall, I threw myself through the hole I made earlier.

With no idea what was on the other side, I tucked and tried to somersault so my feet would come down first. I managed it, sort of, but because what was on the other side turned out to be a pond, landing feet first didn't make much difference. It wasn't deep, but that also didn't make much difference for though the water only came up to my ankles, my momentum was all pitching forward so I could break into a run but the additional drag of water and pond weeds against my leading foot meant I fell forward.

Anastasia Aaronson, possibly the only person on the planet who could wield source energy, carrying God's sword, and tasked with finding a way to save mankind from enslavement by an ancient race of magical beings. Now soaked to the bone and covered in pond scum.

Terrific.

I couldn't stop myself from stealing a glance over my shoulder where I found two dozen faces pressed against the hole I dove through. They all bore the same curious look as if they all wanted to ask why I thought now was a good time for a swim.

Cursing my luck, I shoved off the ground, and dripping dirty water, lily pads and slime, I glooped my way to the bank. Praying I wouldn't find a frog in the front pocket of my hoody later, I started running, though the correct adjective for my particular form of ambulation probably needed the word slosh in it somewhere.

The fireball was still dissipating into the night sky as I ran for the temple wall and the orange glow beneath it let me know a fire still raged. I didn't know what that meant, but my worst fear was confirmed when I heard the zing and sizzle of hellfire being exchanged.

With a shouted apology to anyone who might hear me, I blasted a hole in the ancient temple wall and ran through it. The shotgun bag proved easy to swing around from my back to my front, one easy move presenting the zip and it was in my hand a moment later as I charged through the dust and debris of the wall to emerge in clean air with the sword in my left hand and a sinfire orb in my right ready to go.

What I saw to my utter disbelief was a scene of chaos and destruction. There were bodies strewn on the ground and dark stains that had to be blood seeping from them. Ahead of me, a building was on fire, causing dancing light to fill the gaps between the businesses on either side of the road. I could hear car engines being driven hard and cars colliding with each other as they tried to avoid what stood at the centre of the mess.

There, looking around casually, and with Daniel's limp body lying at their feet were four beings I took to be demons. They could be angels for all I knew but I doubted they were. Angels, the ones I knew at least, were all about preserving life. They still intended to rule humanity, but they believed we would let them do it because it was for the best.

The demons were standing over Daniel. One, a woman by the look of her through the flickering light, even had her foot resting on his head. That they were still here meant they hadn't come for Daniel or, at least, not just for him: they wanted me too.

Well, I wanted Daniel too, so I guessed it was time to fight.

With a platoon of soldiers at my side, a hasty plan would give our attack some shape. That doesn't really work when it's just you, so I gripped the sword tightly in my left hand, powered up my right and strode toward them down the centre of the street.

Walking past bodies on the ground and toward four demons using fire as their backdrop, I felt like I was approaching the gates of hell. Maybe I was, but even though my stomach was curling in fear, I knew this was when I got to find out what I was capable of. I didn't know who these demons were, but they looked better prepared than any I had faced before. They looked like warriors: trained and honed and skilled for their craft. Common sense told me that after killing five of their number, only those who felt the most confident would come after me, or perhaps it was Beelzebub himself who handpicked his best.

Well, best, let's see what you've got.

A swirl of smoke obscured my view of them for a moment just as one spotted me. As the smoke cleared the next moment, all four were looking my way. Predictably, and just as I hoped, they started flinging hellfire my way. I was ready for it; eager might be a better word and the pain that went with the hits didn't seem to bother me the way it did the first few times I experienced it.

Five. Seven. A dozen strikes hit me before they wised up and stopped flinging their primary weapon. The orb I still held in my right hand slowly changed from light blue to a smutty dark red as the hellfire filled it. I could feel the raw power filling my veins as I held it, waiting for them to realise their error and think about what to do next.

Would they go for elemental magic? I didn't give them the chance. The moment they silently questioned their options, I hit them with everything I had. My right leg went back to brace against the outgoing force, and with a scream, I hit them.

The sustained stream of hellfire lifted all four from their feet, tumbling them backward to slam into the building behind them. The building's front façade caved in, brickwork, plaster and glass enveloping the demons as they went through the outer wall.

A surprised chuckle escaped my lips when I dropped the stream. They were all down! In one hit I knocked all four of them back ten yards and through a building. Though I knew it to be premature jubilation, I was shocked to my core when a sword flew from the building to skewer my chest.

It came so fast I had no time to react and just like I had done to them, the kinetic energy in it threw me backwards. I landed on my back in a painfully crumpled heap but looking down my chin, I was shocked to find the sword wasn't sticking out from my chest.

The armour had done its job and now it glowed outside my skin to look like ethereal armour plate. This was marvellous! Ha! Take that demons! You can't kill me. Then I thought about what would have happened if it hit my head or my lower abdomen and wondered how quickly I could find more armour to protect the exposed parts of me.

Daniel was getting up, rolling over onto his front so he could lever himself off the ground. His new suit was destroyed, the bare skin of his right arm and torso showing through where the material had been ripped away. I too got back to my feet, but the demons in the building across the street were fighting their way out.

This was far from over.

Seeing the flashes of light as the four demons in the building began to blast their way clear of the rubble, Daniel jogged over to me. They must have hurt him bad because he was still limping, but he crossed the space as quickly as he could.

'We have to go,' he insisted, lifting his hand to create a portal. I frowned, unsure that was the best tactic, and seeing my hesitance, he grabbed my left arm, 'You cannot beat them, Anastasia! They are Beelzebub's generals. Hand-picked by him for their ruthlessness, cunning, and skill.'

'Really,' I sneered. 'I just knocked them all down with one punch.'

'You got lucky,' Daniel insisted. 'They let you hit them so they could see how strong you are. That is the level of confidence you are dealing with. They won't use hellfire now.'

I'd distracted him for too long and they were coming back out of the building. True to his word, they didn't throw more hellfire my way, but I couldn't see anyone drawing on elemental magic either. They were going to fight me with their weapons instead.

I doubted it was in my best interest to trade blows with them, but I waited to see what they could do. With a hissing snarl that was an order, not a request, I told Daniel to, 'Get behind me and keep firing hellfire into my back.'

'What?'

'Just do it, demon. Don't let up until I tell you to.'

Then I started running toward them. The sword was still in my left hand, and I almost stumbled when Daniel got with the program and hit me with a blast of hellfire. Just like fighting the first bunch of demons two nights ago outside the cathedral in Rochester, I was being reloaded as I fired, and I put it to good use.

My bet was they might be skilled fighters, but they had never faced anything like me before. Also, how skilled can you get when defence isn't something you need to worry about? The four were wise enough to spread out, darting to my left and right which not only divided my focus but meant I couldn't hit them all with one sustained beam of energy.

It also meant I could take them on one to one and that worked nicely for me.

The nearest to me was tall and lean with dark skin. His muscular arms were bare and in them he held a large axe. I could see light from the fire reflecting off the razor-sharp edge, but the moment he held it aloft, I smashed him backward with a stream of hellfire.

I was only five yards from him when my blast hit his face and sent him flying upward and back. He would need a few seconds to recover, and what could I do in that time? The remaining three were shouting instructions to each other but there was no consensus about what to do.

Daniel continued to recharge me with hellfire but, perhaps sensing I had all I needed, he switched target to hit one of the other demons; the female I noted. She didn't go down from the blasts, and even caught the second one but it did a great job of distracting her while I closed the distance between us.

I planned to kill her with the sword, but switching hands meant I lost my ability to fire at them, and that let the other two come at me. The sword powered up, but from nowhere I got slammed from the left and all the air left my lungs.

I should be thankful, I think, that I hit a car because it tumbled me. Unable to fight my change in inertia, I went over the low bonnet of the Japanese sports car to land on the ground on the other side which placed me out of direct line of fire.

It had to have been a manipulation of wind that got me, one of the demons having the sense to attack me from afar. That I had time to come to rest on the ground amid the broken glass and bits of rubble, and then think about the fact that I had, made me question why they hadn't followed up the spell with another more deadly one.

The answer had two parts.

The first part, which I saw when I placed my palm on the car just as a jet of hellfire left my arm, was that Daniel was fighting back. He had some distance from them and two were down. The remaining two wanted to come for me, but as the car sailed end over end to force one of them to drop his particular spell in favour of not getting crushed, I saw a second reason why I was still breathing. Daniel and I were not the only ones fighting.

In fact, there were now two further problems for the demons to tackle. The police, who chose to arrive without sirens and were firing hand-guns at the demons, for all the difference it made, and beyond the demons, a lone figure standing on a low rooftop to rain sinfire down on them.

Chapter 17

I knew who it was in my first glance: Benjamin. He was an angel about whom my feelings were still ambiguous. Supposedly a good guy, he'd left me to fight for my life against a squad of shilt while my amputated stumps bled onto the floor. He then did it again the first time I met Daniel and I punched him in the face for it.

How Benjamin might have found me was a question for another time. The demons had found me too, so I was leaving a trail somehow, but the point was the attacking force of four well-trained demons now faced impossible odds.

Or so I thought.

In the next second, I heard a grunt from my left and was shocked to see Daniel struggling with an axe that appeared to have grown from his chest. I hadn't seen it be thrown but the demon who had been recharging me with hellfire was out of the fight for now. Before I could react to that, a gout of flame hit the leading edge of the police. They were not all in one place, indeed they had come from several directions but the glut of them were funnelled into a street where the death toll and casualty rate would be high.

Then Benjamin vanished from sight as a combination of hellfire and lightning ripped into the building beneath his feet. The four demons were able to turn the tide in the space of two heartbeats. That should be the space of two resting heartbeats because mine was pumping like crazy.

With the car I rolled over now out of my way, I was exposed on all sides. The demons, though fanned out, were ahead of me covering an arc that was perhaps sixty degrees of a circle. The police posed as much threat, if not more, for I felt sure they would shoot me if they got the chance. Those in different directions to the poor souls set alight by the demons' fire attack were shouting orders and instructions, none of which I could understand. But I knew what they meant when a bullet hit my armour, forcing me to duck.

This was a deadly environment to stay in, and I no longer had the upper hand. Daniel's situation looked desperate; I had to get to him before he chose to open a portal and save himself. Keeping low, so I could skirt along the cars, I knew I was in trouble when my hair started to lift. Any second now, lightning was going to toast me and that could be game over, magical armour and sword of God notwithstanding.

I threw myself the rest of the way to the surface of the street and rolled onto my back so I could fire while minimising the size of the target they had to hit. I couldn't see them though. None were in sight, and when the lightning came it was from behind me – the opposite direction to the demons.

Seeing the blinding flash go over me and not into my body, I rolled back to my front to make a run for Daniel, but there now was Benjamin, tearing the axe from Daniel's chest with both hands. Hellfire rained in their direction, hitting them both, but all I had to do was sidestep to place myself into the salvo. Too late, the demons saw me and stopped firing but not before I absorbed several hits. I quickly spindled the energy inside my body and held the sword out in both hands as I faced down the demon posse.

I was ready to call it a draw, backing toward Daniel and Benjamin and hoping they were ready to get out of here. Unperturbed, the demons advanced. They were taking shots from the police the whole time, bullets knocking small chunks of flesh from their bodies as they stalked toward me.

'Guys?' I shouted.

A hand touched my neck and I felt the pull of the portal behind me.

'I've got you,' Daniel gasped, still not fully recovered from his injuries.

Safety beckoned but just as we started to go through, a stray round clipped my left shoulder, flipping me out of Daniel's grip. I tumbled to the floor in dire agony, a feeling like fire searing where the bullet tore the flesh of my shoulder open.

Panicking, I looked up to see the portal close. Daniel and Benjamin were gone, and that left me alone with the four nightmarish demons. It came as little surprise when a lance of lightning arced down, and all my buttons got turned to off.

Chapter 18
The SIA

In his private office, deep beneath London's Canary Wharf, Commissioner Michael Swinton was not enjoying a phone call. It was with his immediate superior in Washington DC, a man Swinton learned to loathe seconds after meeting him for the first time. According to rumour, he was loved by his fellow countrymen in the US division of the SIA and had been a war hero in Iraq in the nineties. Swinton thought Colt Ironbolt was an intolerable bore. I mean, seriously, what kind of name is Colt Ironbolt? It's like someone was writing a superhero book and needed something ridiculous for the hero's alter ego.

'Why did you send two supers to America?' Ironbolt demanded, and in his usual style he then answered his own question before Swinton got a chance. 'Because you failed to think, Commissioner. That's why. Ignoring any concerns about budget, which I will add, are a concern, your men arrived ten hours after the event was over. What are they still doing on US soil?'

'They acted without authority,' Swinton replied. It was true that they had elected to go to America without expressing any intention to do so, but technically, he gave them authority when he sent them after Anastasia Aaronson. He'd been leaned on hard enough that Swinton thought he would be happy no matter what they did, so long as they could show a result or, at least, some progress. He hadn't thought they would use the issued credit cards to board a plane to the states where the SIA already had more agents than anywhere else on the planet.

Swinton opened his mouth to elaborate on what he now intended to do, but Ironbolt cut him off again. 'Well, that's just about the goddamndest thing I've heard you say to date, Swinton. They're your men. They do what you tell them. Whatever they do, it's down to you, so whether you sent them here or they chose to come because they thought it met with your instructions or lack thereof, it's still down to you.'

'Yes, sir. I am perfectly aware of that ...'

'Well get that thumb out of your ass and find the girl! She's British! This is a task for the Brits. Goddamn it!'

The line went dead, leaving Swinton to stare at the handset accusingly. He really loathed having anyone give him orders. Hated it, in fact. After three deep breaths to still his pulse, he pressed the button to connect his phone to his assistant in the outer office. Margaret was the sort of stern woman one found working as a personal assistant all over the planet. She would organise the executive's life, arrange all manner of aspects that got in the way of them remaining focussed on the task of doing their job, and in an unspoken way, ruled over them with an iron rod. People wanting to see the executive had to first get past the Margarets of the world and that was a tougher task than most wanted to bother with. It whittled down the field to those who truly had business the executive needed to hear.

'Margaret can you patch me through to Crockett and Tubbs, please?'

'Of course, Mr Swinton,' she replied curtly, performing the task while questioning why the man couldn't dial his own phone.

In his office, staring blankly at the wall opposite his desk and wondering what he might have done to deserve all this grief, Commissioner Swinton listened to the phone begin to ring. It rang on for some time before it was finally answered.

'Garfield.' The single word gave Swinton a new problem because now he couldn't remember which one of the pair Garfield was. Was he Crockett or Tubbs?

'This is Commissioner Swinton,' he growled, deciding it didn't matter which of the two he was addressing. 'What are you doing in America?'

At the other end, Garfield, a tall man whose grandparents came to England from Jamaica in the fifties, had the phone on speaker so his partner could also hear whatever nonsense their boss was going to spew.

Sitting next to him, in the Volvo they hired, was Marcus Riddle. He was a shifter, just like Garfield but compared to Garfield's deep coffee-coloured skin, he was whiter than white to the point that his tan-free skin had an almost see-through tinge. Hearing the commissioner's question, he shook his head sadly.

'You told us to find the girl, sir.' Riddle pointed out. 'This is where the trail starts. We have to begin at the beginning. That's why it's called picking up a trail.'

Hearing the sarcastic retort from a subordinate on top of the rebuke he just suffered from his own superior, Swinton blew his stack.

Garfield thumbed the speaker button on the phone but didn't pick it up. The commissioner's voice could be heard but they were now unable to make out what he was saying and had no interest either. Both men picked up their coffee cups to drink while their boss went on a thirty second rant.

Only when it subsided, and they could hear him speaking at a normal volume, did Garfield press the speaker button again.

The commissioner's voice cut back in at an audible volume halfway through a sentence '... you hear what I said?'

Both men frowned. Riddle said, 'No, sir. Could you say that again, please?'

In his office, Swinton bit the handset of his phone and mimed strangling it. He wanted to be a supervillain who had self-destruct buttons fitted to his underlings so he could literally fire them when they displeased him.

Managing to speak calmly even through gritted teeth, Swinton said, 'I want you on the next plane back to England.'

'You don't want us to catch the girl?' Garfield questioned, unable to believe what he was hearing.

Exploding again, Swinton raged, 'You haven't got any idea where she is! I've just read a report that makes it sound like she might be in Japan! Are you planning to go there next?'

Aggravating his boss by supplying sensible responses in a calm and rational manner, Riddle said, 'No, sir. Our plan was to stay here where her friends are and wait until she returns.'

The statement stopped Swinton's next salvo of insults just as they were leaving his mouth. 'Her friends are there? What friends?' Was there a thin ray of hope here?

Not bothering to answer Swinton's questions, Riddle told him. 'The incident at the cathedral wasn't the only event last night. On the street opposite, eyewitnesses reported a blonde woman floating three feet off the ground while a handsome and well-dressed man in a dark suit threw dark red balls of light at her.'

Swinton frowned. 'So? So what? That sounds like a demon having a fight with someone who is not Anastasia Aaronson. Get to the point, man.'

Garfield couldn't keep the bored tone from his voice when he cut in, 'We found footage of the woman and it looks like the one Schneider rescued. The one he brought back to the facility in Bremen. I remember her because she is so hot. And the well-dressed demon sounds just like the same one in the police report from the Rochester jail break when Aaronson escaped.'

Swinton's eyes flared. 'Tell me you've got something, and you are not just guessing.'

Garfield flipped his eyes at his partner. They both thought the commissioner was a buffoon. 'The woman's name is Ayla Pendragon. She is the daughter of a senator. Finding her address was easy so we are staking out her place to see if we can spot Aaronson. No sign of her yet, but the cop is here, so we think she might be using this place as a base.'

'Cop? What cop?'

'Um ...' Garfield had to dig through his notes to find the name. 'He was the arresting officer in Rochester ... here it is, Detective Sergeant Ralph Spencer. He comes outside for a smoke at least once an hour. It's definitely him and he is at the home of a senator's daughter who we can directly link to Otto Schneider.'

'Who we can directly link to Anastasia Aaronson,' finished Swinton, punching the air like he'd just scored a goal. 'Look, forget what I said earlier about coming back to England.' Garfield and Riddle both pulled faces because they hadn't bothered to listen to that bit, 'stay there, report your findings, and when you can be sure she is there, I want you to get her.'

'By force?' Riddle sought to confirm.

'You still have the tranquiliser guns?'

'Yes.'

'That's what they are for. Put her down and take her directly to the nearest SIA facility in New York.'

'We have the address,' confirmed Garfield.

Swinton pursed his lips and took a second to question whether he needed to say anything else before he ended the call. Unable to think of anything he exhaled through his nose and said, 'Well done, chaps. This is good work.'

Garfield threw his hands in the air. It wasn't good work! They tracked their target across the world and found her likely base of operations in under twelve hours. James Bond couldn't do better. It was incredible work.

Shaking his head while he spoke, Riddle said, 'Thank you, sir. We will report back when we have her.'

Chapter 19

The portal spilled Daniel and Benjamin onto the dirt in the immortal realm. Both had seen the bullet strike Anastasia and watched her fall as the portal closed with her still on Earth.

Benjamin screamed his rage and began to open a portal. He had to get back before Beelzebub's general got to her.

Daniel, still recovering from his wounds, covered in blood, and wearing brand new clothes now reduced to rags, wasn't going to let any of that prevent him from being the one to get back to the mortal realm first. That Benjamin had found them in Japan disturbed him greatly. What did he want?

Two separate portals opened, both the angel and demon stepped into them and arrived mere yards apart back in the debris-strewn street in Osaka. Fire still raged in the street ahead and sirens wailed as more police arrived to support those already there. However, the shouting, wailing from wounded, and roar of the fire couldn't mask the fact that the four demons were no longer anywhere to be seen. And neither was Anastasia.

Benjamin turned to ask Daniel where they would take her, but before he could speak, the angry demon threw a bolt of hellfire. It hit Benjamin's chest at close range and threw him backward into a car. He left a dent in the door, but even falling to his knees as he rebounded, he summoned source energy and gave back as good as he got.

Daniel, filled with rage that Beelzebub had taken Ana so easily, wanted someone to blame and the angel made a perfect target. He was following up with a second blast of hellfire when Benjamin's orb of sinfire hit him square in the face.

A shout told them the cops were about to fire, but both ignored the insignificant humans as they went at each other hand to hand. What humans would refer to as street fighting was all but alien to the magical race of angels and demons. They relied on source energy or elemental magic to inflict damage or defend themselves. However, Daniel was so close that when Benjamin regained his feet, he threw a punch to the demon's gut.

It was followed by an experimental kick to Daniel's ribs and then a haymaker punch that might have knocked the demon from his feet if it had connected. As it was, he missed wildly and swung around through a hundred and eighty degrees to show Daniel his back.

Daniel, shocked that the angel would resort to physical violence, chose to return the favour. Now that Benjamin was all twisted up and facing the wrong way, he lifted his right foot, and kicked out to boot the angel in the butt.

Benjamin shot forward, colliding with the side of the car again, but pushed away and swung a hard right fist backward in an arc that connected with Daniel's jaw.

It was a glancing blow that shocked the demon but did little to prevent him slamming the angel back again as he threw his bodyweight forward. The two scrappers were being watched by a dozen police officers. All had their weapons aimed but none could believe what they were seeing and were waiting for their captain to give an order.

The captain wanted to just shoot both men. Truthfully, he didn't think they were men. He'd just seen them produce balls of light from their hands, but they looked like men and they moved like men. He couldn't shoot them though and currently there seemed to be no danger to life. However, doing nothing wasn't an option either so he would have to send men forward to physically restrain the two idiots doing a terrible job of fighting each other.

'I came to help,' wheezed Benjamin while Daniel tried to throttle him. A sharp elbow to the demon's ribs broke his hold and allowed the angel to get enough space to lash out with a kick.

Daniel parried the kick away with a hand as he sneered, 'You came to take her away from me. We were doing fine. You just want the sword and armour.'

'And what do you want her for?' demanded Benjamin, throwing his arms forward to grapple with the demon. They ended up hugging each other as each tried to throw the other to the ground. 'All you have done for hundreds of years is enslave humans, Daniel. I saw you on the battlefield,' Benjamin stopped speaking for a moment when the demon slammed him into another car and knocked the air from his lungs. 'You were at Beelzebub's feet. Have you fallen from favour? Do you plan to regain it by giving the armour to Beelzebub? The demons must not rule the Earth.'

'Oh, because the angels will do so much of a better job?' Daniel got the words out before Benjamin struck between his legs with a knee.

Benjamin laughed as the demon sagged. 'Ha! Immortal or not, that's still got to hurt!'

In his moment of jubilation, Benjamin didn't see Daniel's fist close, and the uppercut delivered directly to the angel's groin as the demon fell to his knees, put them both in the same position.

The police captain snorted with laughter. 'Just get them,' he told his officers with a casually waved arm.

Daniel saw the humans coming, most holding their pathetic guns up as if they could do him any harm, but others produced steel cuffs they clearly proposed to restrain him with. He didn't have time for this; he needed to get back to hell and find where they took Anastasia. Though he felt like vomiting from the unusual pain in his core, he lifted his left hand to open a portal.

As the air immediately behind him began to shimmer, he grabbed the angel with his other hand. 'You owe me,' he snapped, pulling Benjamin after him as he let his body fall backward and into the immortal realm.

Chapter 20

Hitting the floor jolted me back to consciousness and I was shocked to find the sword still gripped in my left hand. My body was a ball of pain from the lightning strike, but it was my left shoulder that screamed the loudest. A glance revealed the tattered flesh where the bullet tore through my deltoid to expose the meat inside.

I felt sick but when I heard a voice shout, 'Get the sword,' adrenalin kicked in and I had to fight whether I was going to throw up or not.

I was on my knees and hunched over so my forehead almost touched the cool marble floor. The sword was under my body and the demons were coming for me right now.

Instinctively, I rolled right, protecting my left shoulder, and screaming against the pain, I thrust upward from the floor with the sword.

One of the demons, the dark-skinned one, was coming down to rip the weapon from my grasp and got it straight between his ribs. It went right through him, but I held it in my left hand and couldn't push source energy through the sword to kill him. All I needed to do was switch hands, but in the second it took to do that, I got blasted by a second demon, this time the female, who was right there next to me on the floor.

The next few seconds became a melee of arms, legs, the swinging sword, and errant hellfire as I flung energy in every direction. The female hit me with hellfire to stop me killing the demon I stuck the sword through, and that recharged me briefly, but they had learned quickly not to use source energy on me because it just made me stronger. I knew they could throw flame my way, and quite frankly I was terrified they would, but when none came, I had to guess it was because they needed me alive.

I was inside a building, but other than that, and the certainty of being in hell, I could be anywhere. The floor was shiny, fawn-coloured marble, the walls marble too but in a shade closer to white. The ceiling was high above my head, perhaps double the height of a standard room in a house and there were no windows. There was a large vase in one corner, and by large, I mean I could hide inside it and have room to play the violin. Otherwise, the room was devoid of features save for two doors in adjacent walls.

I took all that in during a second of respite. The demons were circling me, keeping their distance because I had the sword in my right hand, and it was powered up for battle. The first one to get within striking distance was going to die, even if that cost me my own life. The only problem with that was they could see me weakening. Judging by the amount of blood on the floor, my wound was leaking enough to render me unconscious soon. My left arm was already useless, hanging limply at my side and too painful to consider lifting again.

I was a wounded animal; backed into a corner with nothing to lose and no chance of survival. All the predators needed to do was wait, and that was what they were doing. Well, that and constantly probing me with elemental magic which they used to push me around, wind spells buffeting me.

My breath came in heaving lumps as I growled in defiance. Little spots were beginning to dance in front of my eyes from the blood loss. I didn't have long and when I fell, they would kill me. The sword would be theirs, the armour too.

I had failed completely.

Drawing in a shuddering breath, I bunched my shaking muscles in preparation. If I was going to die, then I was going to take one of them with me. Every demon I killed was one less horror for the Earth to suffer. The female was my target; something about her smile made me want to make it stop. Their circling had placed her behind me, but I was about to spin and lunge. I would have to cover three or four yards to get to her, but if there is any justice in the cosmos, a person's dying effort ought to be successful.

I feigned forward, then changed direction and spun off my rear foot to run at her. Raising the sword as I turned, a hand came from nowhere to grab my right wrist and caught me completely by surprise. The hand yanked me off the ground, whipping me around until I slammed face first into a block of solid muscle from which I rebounded. The sword was plucked from my grip as I fell away to land painfully. Back on the floor, I looked up to find myself now sprawled at Beelzebub's feet.

I never even sensed him enter the room.

Looking down at me from far above, the demons' ruler said, 'You are hurt, Anastasia.' I think he said something else, but the banging noise in my head became too much and the sparkly lights all kind of merged into one and went black.

Chapter 21

Back in the immortal realm again, Daniel opened his left hand and used his right foot to shove the angel away. He was mad as hell and wanted to vent his anger by stomping the angel into the ground. He knew they were evenly matched though; Benjamin was the angel who most regularly got in his way on Earth.

Over the last few centuries, ever since Daniel started his quest to find familiars, he and Benjamin had clashed many times. Benjamin would consider himself the victor in those encounters, Daniel knew, because more often than not, the angel's arrival prevented him from taking the familiar he was there for. Sometimes, he would come back for another attempt at a later date, but often as not, he would move on – there were more targets than time would allow.

He got to his feet as quickly as he could, but no quicker than the angel so both came back into wary poses that suggested they could resume fighting straight away if the other showed the slightest sign that it was their intention.

'What now?' asked Benjamin, watching the demon closely.

Daniel frowned deeply. 'What do you mean, what now? How about you go back to the angels' camp and never bother me again. What were you doing in Japan anyway?'

Benjamin ran possible answers through his head quickly. The truth was always the best option. 'I was there to get the sword.'

Daniel snorted a breath through his nose. 'Well, you failed. Beelzebub must have it by now. Unless the generals are all planning to betray and murder him, which I doubt, then he sent them to get it.'

The demon started to walk away but Benjamin got in his way. 'Then we have to go after Anastasia and rescue her and the sword.'

Daniel frowned even more deeply. 'We?'

'I saw what happened to you when Nathaniel was killed. What is your plan? You are outcast from the demons. They probably blame you for Nathaniel's death.' Daniel turned away again and when Benjamin caught his arm, he snatched it free and pushed hellfire into the other hand as a warning.

'Don't touch me, angel.'

Benjamin kept his own hands visible and empty. 'She has some of the armour, doesn't she? You were helping her get it. Tell me why.'

Daniel almost spat a curt response at the angel, but something held him back. Why had he been helping her? His plan was to help her get the armour, seduce her slowly until she trusted him completely and then betray her, handing her over to Beelzebub as a demonstration of his true allegiance. The effort of multiple millennia had all been about getting up the ladder to sit by the ruler's right hand. Was the opportunity gone? He wasn't sure, but if it were, then he still needed to get to Anastasia and get the armour because the only way he could survive was if by some miracle the humans could win.

It was ridiculous though. Nothing could stand up to the might Beelzebub had assembled. So, where did that leave him?

'Only she can get the armour,' he grumbled his answer eventually. 'None of us, demon or angel, can go into the religious places where your leader stupidly had the humans stash the weapons and other artefacts. And any mortal who attempts to retrieve it will surely die. Finding her took hundreds of years. In truth, I never expected to find anyone who could retrieve the artefacts and had all but given up on it when the shilt reported her ability.'

Benjamin narrowed his eyes at the demon. 'If the demons have her, she must be rescued. If they use her to get the rest of the pieces, Beelzebub will become invincible. You don't have to be on the angels' side to see why that is bad. What will happen to you when the death curse fails? You will not be allowed to exist outside of the demon collective.'

Daniel looked down at his tattered suit. He wanted to argue, but the angel was right, and he knew it. Losing Anastasia sealed his fate. He could hide, but the best he could hope for was a slightly prolonged, but pitiful life. They would find him eventually. His only bargaining chip had been taken from him.

While the demon contemplated his fate, Benjamin accepted what he needed to do. The only question was whether he could convince Godfrey to agree to a raid, or if it were foolhardy to attempt such a strategy when there were others who would gladly go behind Godfrey's back to join him. Involve their leader and risk being told no when he felt certain going after the sword was the only choice or mount a mutiny now before Godfrey could steer them all to a defeat many believed was coming.

Making a decision, he closed his eyes and prayed history would forgive him. When he opened them again, the demon was gone, no trace left to show that he had ever been there. For one moment, Benjamin had thought the demon might join him. Daniel would have been useful in the quest to retrieve the sword and the girl. Too late now, Benjamin opened a portal and stepped through it.

Chapter 22

I awoke with a dry mouth and a strange feeling of detachment from my body. Where was the pain I felt before? With a jolt, I remembered Beelzebub taking the sword and sat up from my prone position as if the bed I lay on were suddenly electrified.

I froze instantly as the lord of hell looked my way. He was sitting at a desk across the room, and after glancing across to me, he went back to what he was doing.

'I'm glad to see you are recovered,' he commented, his eyes looking down at the desk where I could now see he was inspecting his father's sword.

I looked across to my left shoulder and noticed two things: it was healed, and I wasn't wearing the same clothes I had been. My prosthetic left forearm and hand was fitted incorrectly which told me it had been taken off and put back on while I was unconscious. The artificial limb worked by interpreting electrical impulses in the muscles of my arm, but it wasn't doing anything at the moment. I unclipped the latches that kept it in place, adjusted and refitted it while holding the hand toward the ceiling. My left index finger, which I was moving in my head, came to life all of a sudden, twitching back and forth under my control. Satisfied, I craned my head to get a better look at my shoulder.

Where the bullet had ripped away flesh, neat pink skin could now be seen with no trace of a scar. I frowned slightly because I used to have a birthmark there and it was strangely absent now. Rolling my shoulder, I confirmed it felt as good as new, then inspected my clothes.

On the bed, there was no cover over me, so I could see my legs were clad in rough brown leather trousers. I use the word rough to describe the outer effect, not the feel against my skin, which was supple, soft, and cool. I had never worn leather next to my skin before and it felt kind of odd in a sexual way. The skin of my middle was exposed and my belly button, which I have never liked, was on display for the world to see because the trousers had a hipster design that stopped two inches lower than I would normally wear a pair of jeans, and my top was little more than a bra with some extra material. It wouldn't stretch down to cover my belly and it made me feel like I needed to go back in time and do more sit ups.

Above the brown leather trousers, I had a sort of cropped tank top made of a dark red cotton and over that ... honestly, I don't know what you call it. It was a leather device to pull my boobs in and shove them up. It might have been great for a teenage boy's bedroom wall poster if worn by a busty girl, but I can boast a double A cup so shoving and squeezing has little effect. Like a bra worn on the outside, it went right around me and over my shoulders and had a half cup that sat under my boobs like a shelf but didn't extent far enough up to cover my nipples which I could see through the cotton of the tank top beneath.

I felt on display.

Looking over the edge of the bed, I found knee-high boots with a chunky heel. They were brown to match the trousers and laced up the outside. I wanted to ask where the heck they found clothes my size and what might have happened to the clothes I had been wearing. Other questions had to take precedence though.

'Where am I?' I asked as an opening gambit to see if the giant demon wanted to talk.

'My private chambers,' replied Beelzebub without looking my way. 'I trust the clothes are a comfortable fit. It was ... a test to find items your size.'

I guess that's why I look like a wannabe vampire slayer from a teenage boy's wet dream then. I kept that thought to myself and slid off the bed to put the boots on.

'They fit fine,' I replied, carefully not thanking him since I was his captive and we were not on friendly terms. 'Why am I here?'

Now he did look my way, swivelling first one, then the other tree trunk thick leg around so he faced me. He didn't get up, which meant his head was at roughly the same height as mine. 'You have something I want,' he replied, his voice a rumbling deep bass. 'My father's armour is anchored to your body and must be freely given; I cannot take it.'

'Unlike the sword,' I commented.

'Yes.' He reached around to pick the gleaming black blade from the desk. It looked tiny in his hand and against his body whereas it dwarfed me. 'I wish to express my thanks for returning this to me.' He raised a hand to stop me saying anything in response. 'I know that was not your intention, but it has been a long time since I last saw this sword and I am pleased to hold it again regardless of the circumstances that brought it back to me.'

Wonderful. The lord of darkness is holding a deadly weapon with which he can finally kill his brother, the angels and anyone else he cares to stab with it, and I am the one getting thanked for its safe delivery. Perfect.

Already bored, I asked. 'So what now? What if I deny you the armour?'

He got to his feet, his imposing presence making me want to back up a pace or twelve. My feet twitched but I refused to let them move. Coming closer, he said, 'If I intended to take the armour from you by force, I would not have bothered to heal you. I could have let you die, and the armour would have freed itself. You are too precious for that to be your fate, Anastasia. You may be far more important than you know.' All the while he was talking, he kept advancing, the sword in his right hand, but he stopped a respectful distance away and looked down at me with eyes that held a tenderness that seemed out of place. 'I want you to join me, Anastasia.'

I almost choked.

'Join with me,' he insisted, 'and help me to save countless human lives.' When I narrowed my eyes at him in a challenge, he continued. 'The war has to come, Anastasia. Nothing can prevent that. My father's death curse will fail and when it does, all my kind will arrive back on Earth. Living in harmony with humanity is not an option. We will rule over them and reset the Earth to a sustainable balance after the centuries of abuse and neglect. How many must die in that process will be up to mankind to decide. With humans to speak on my behalf, perhaps we can end the fighting sooner rather than later.'

He made a strong argument, but I suspected the alternative to agreeing was terrible torture and endless agony. He hadn't asked a question yet, so he didn't get an answer from me. He got a question instead. 'You didn't kill your father, did you?'

I caught him off guard; he hadn't been expecting it and he raised his right eyebrow as a show of surprise. 'No,' he confirmed. 'That was my brother. I saw him leaving my father's chambers but before I could challenge him, the death curse took effect and Godfrey was swift to blame me for all that followed. It was a lie that was easy to believe because I was staunchly against my father's policies. It saddens me that I was right, and the humans did require firmer treatment.' He hung his head. 'That my father had to die to prove my point remains a tragedy.'

The sword was tantalisingly close to me. I knew I could use it to kill him if I had control of it. How to get it though? Slip off my top and lure him into bed, then kill him when he is sleeping? An unlikely scenario even if I didn't have a face like an industrial accident. Blast him with sinfire, grab the sword and kill him? Even less likely than the first idea.

Taking Beelzebub out of the equation sounded like a great idea. It would most likely throw the demons into utter disarray, but then what? Someone else would step up to take on the mantle of leadership. Would they be strong enough to wield the sword? I didn't know how many of demon kind were able to create the sustained stream the weapon required; I just knew the ability was rare. Assuming a new leader did arise, would they be better or worse than the one before me now.

And what of the angels? They would hear of the power vacuum - would they strike? My next assumption that they would, led me to question what would follow. Godfrey still planned to rule the Earth but with fewer human casualties. That sounded good, but I only had his word that he wouldn't slaughter billions, and truthfully, I believed Beelzebub about who his father's true murderer was.

My attention came back to the present when my oh so pleasant (for now) captor said, 'I await an answer to my question, Anastasia.'

I looked up at him. And when I say looked up you can believe I had to crane my neck. 'You are going to have to be more specific about what it is you want me to do, Bub,' I shortened his name for my own amusement. 'Your request that I join with you seems to have a lot of grey area in it.'

His face was so far above mine I was having trouble working out if he looked annoyed or not, but I tensed myself to dart backwards just in case anyway. Would he stab me with the sword and then heal me just to teach me some manners?

I needn't have worried though for he tipped his head back to let out a deep belly laugh. When he stopped and his gaze returned to my face, he said, 'I wondered what to expect of you, Anastasia. Your dimensions are childlike, yet you speak and act like a seasoned warrior and have the skills to back it up.' I wasn't sure I would make the same observation of myself. 'I will grant you certain liberties, Anastasia. I will ensure persons dear to you are spared from any harm. As many as you want, but you cannot claim a continent or a country. I will, however, grant you a region and that region shall be your fiefdom in the new world. You will be one of very few non-demons to be given a place to rule. The humans in your territory will be yours to rule over and you will answer only to me. In return, I demand that you do my bidding until the death curse fails and when it does, you will fight on my side against the humans and the angels foolish enough to oppose me.'

He believed what he was offering was a deal I could accept. I dipped my head to make it look like I was giving his offer some thought but what was going through my mind was a series of questions to get me to why he would make such an offer. He could just kill me. Couldn't he? I was mortal, the bullet through my shoulder proved that clearly enough. He didn't have to grant me a fiefdom, he certainly didn't need me to help swell his numbers for the war to come. Then it hit me. The thing I could do that no one else could.

'You want me to get the rest of the armour,' I stated, looking back up at him.

His eyes didn't even blink. 'You are very perceptive, Anastasia. Your first task is to return to Earth and obtain the remaining pieces of my father's armour. I do not know if there is anyone else like you anywhere in the mortal realm. Or if there ever has been. My brother believed he was placing our father's sword and armour out of reach and out of his temptation. Had he any sense he would have retained it for himself for that might have tipped the balance slightly in his favour. Now that I have the sword, I must have the armour too and you will retrieve it for me.'

'I don't know where it is,' I answered truthfully.

'And yet you already found two locations and have several pieces,' he countered. 'My generals will travel with you. You will collect the armour and bring it to me.'

I asked a big question, 'And if I refuse?'

He leaned forward at the waist, lowering his head until his face was inches from mine. 'I hope you can see the benefits in being on the winning side, Anastasia. It ought to be motivation enough. However, I am prepared to add additional motivation should it prove necessary.' I felt my stomach tighten. 'You have suffered terrible injuries, Anastasia.' He paused to make sure I was paying attention. 'I can hurt you far worse than you can believe, and you will never die because I will keep healing you.' The image in my mind made my head swim. He straightened to his full height suddenly. 'What is it to be, Anastasia? Eternal torment or a place in my court with protection for those you hold dear.'

A snort of laughter escaped my lips though there was nothing funny about any of this. 'Now that I have no choice, why are you even asking?'

'Because you do have a choice.' He inclined his head. 'I acknowledge that it is not a good one. However, while I may convince you, I cannot compel you; no manipulation of source energy or elemental magic will affect free will. I could torture you into giving me the armour you already have, but I believe you will freely surrender it and I leave it in your possession to provide you with protection in your quest to get the remaining pieces.'

'You're letting me keep the armour?'

'For now.'

'Can I have the sword?'

He moved so fast I didn't have time to react until it was way too late to do anything to defend myself. The sword ignited as Beelzebub pushed source energy into it and he swung it upward at my neck. In panic, I back peddled, but collided with the edge of the bed, bounced off, and still going backward to get away, I fell. He kept coming, following me down to place one giant knee on the floor. His leg was almost as wide as my chest! The sword, which I was seeing in operation from the wrong end for the first time, came to rest a quarter inch from my neck. I swear I could feel the source energy sparking along its outer edge tickling the fine hairs on my skin.

I had asked for the sword, but I no longer wanted it.

'I would kill one of my own for speaking to me the way you chose to. You will leave here now, and you will not stop until you have all that I desire.'

As if hearing a signal I could not, the four generals entered Beelzebub's private chamber, lining up behind him looking much the same as they had in Osaka save for a few clothing changes.

Beelzebub pushed off the floor to stand upright, withdrawing his energy from the sword so it returned to its usual glossy black finish. 'You are well rested?' he addressed the four demons assembled and waiting his command.

They all replied with various positives and superlatives and no one paid any attention to the feeble human on the floor where the lord of hell left her. Anger bubbled and burbled inside me unable to accept the feeling of impotence. I was just one scrap of a human girl with missing parts, but I was going to get them. Oh, I was going to get them good.

Chapter 23

'What do we do if she doesn't come back?' asked Riddle. He was already distinctly bored sitting in the car. He and Garfield were both ex cops recruited by the SIA when they were identified as having qualities that qualified them to work in a newly opened branch of the police. They didn't know each other beforehand but were recruited just weeks apart and met during the additional training they had to undertake. Quite how they had been identified as supernaturals had never been explained, but the SIA knew what they were, and it was that 'special quality' that got them both in.

'She will,' replied Garfield confidently.

Riddle frowned. 'It's been hours,'

'It's still daylight. The demon cannot return yet.'

Riddle gave himself a mental head slap for missing that part. No one seemed to know why demons only appeared at night, but it was an accepted fact. He checked his watch. It was coming up on three in the afternoon and the sun would begin setting soon. His stomach gave a light rumble, but the need to eat was less than the need to get up and move about; hours of inactivity had made him stiff and uncomfortable.

'If we've got a little time, I'm going for a walk,' he announced.

Garfield continued to stare at the house across the street. 'Just don't let them see you,' he warned.

Riddle didn't think his partner needed to remind him of the need for stealth. It wasn't his first stakeout. He let it go. 'Hey, you want anything? I'm going back to that gas station we passed. They had a sandwich joint inside.'

Pursing his lips, Garfield thought about whether he should eat or not. 'Meatball sub?' Probably better to eat now than wait until he was really hungry and didn't dare leave for fear of missing their target.

Riddle nodded and walked away, glad to be out of the car even if it was only for a short while.

Across the street Detective Sergeant Spencer took a cigarette from his packet.

'Another one, dude?' asked Anton, shocked at how much the man smoked. He didn't do it in the house, but it made little difference to the smell coming off the man's clothes, skin, hair, and breath.

'I want to check on our friends across the street,' he replied in a bored tone. He felt like a fifth wheel. Stuck in someone else's house, unable to offer anything much that would be of assistance, and generally feeling in the way, the one thing he had done was point out the car across the street with two men sitting in it.

Ayla calmed his panic that it might be demons because, according to his host, it wouldn't occur to them to not just blow the front door off its hinges and storm the house, plus demons cannot be out in sunlight. Letting his heartrate return to normal, his next assumption was they had to be cops - he recognised a stakeout when he saw one. They had been out there most of the day which meant they would be getting bored and irritable, but also that they were waiting for something and he suspected it was sign of Anastasia.

They were all waiting for that.

He pulled the front door open while slipping on his jacket and made sure the door was closed before lighting his cigarette – the lady of the house had already berated him once for allowing smoke to trail inside her abode where her children might smell it. That they were at school today wasn't an argument he felt worthy of raising.

Pulling his jacket tight about his body – his coat went to Anastasia and got destroyed swiftly thereafter – he blew a stream of smoke into the air and stole a single furtive glance at the car across the street.

Only one man was visible this time, the chap in the driver's seat. The other DS Spencer saw, was walking away down the street. From his knowledge of stakeouts, it was either a bathroom break or a quick pitstop for food. Most likely both to combine tasks. Making a snap decision, despite the cold outside, he took another draw of foul air and set off down the street to see where the other man was going.

THE ARMOUR OF GOD

Chapter 24

Benjamin stole into the angels' camp. His absence would have been noticed by someone, possibly even by everyone, his paranoia told him. He had been loyal to Godfrey his entire life, and until just a few hours ago, he would have argued vehemently that nothing could ever shift his allegiance. However, when he saw the angel's leader demonstrate his dominance over Giannis, Benjamin questioned, for the first time, why it was that he had never questioned his loyalty before.

Was Godfrey the right one to lead them? His family had led the race for generations. Almost as far back as history was written, one of Godfrey's line had been the leader, but it was a leadership based on dominance. His line was the most powerful. Godfrey, his brother Beelzebub, and their father possessed abilities very few others ever had, and none could produce as much power. The sword lived in infamy. It was rarely seen, certainly Benjamin had never seen it, and that was because Godfrey's father didn't feel he needed to wear the armour or carry the sword.

Godfrey wanted to continue that, but his determination to stick to the concept that the armour and sword were best left out of the equation had already backfired. Beelzebub's generals had come for the girl and overwhelmed her. It meant Beelzebub had the sword now. It wasn't just the sword though. Giannis and others were right that Anastasia would go after the armour. Godfrey didn't want to hear it. How could she go after the armour? How would she have any idea how to find it? As much as anything, it was Godfrey's willingness to dismiss the notion that the human girl could create a shift in the balance of things that drove Benjamin to seek her out.

Now he was trying to go unnoticed while also trying to find the angels he needed to speak with. Movement ahead made him pause, ducking slightly to conceal himself while worrying his furtive movements might attract attention more swiftly than brazenly walking through camp. He wanted to avoid meeting Godfrey, but Godfrey would know Benjamin had left the camp and that meant he also needed to avoid at least half of the other angels because Godfrey would have asked them to report when they saw him.

Not in a manner that would make it seem like they were informing on Benjamin. No, Godfrey would make it sound like he hoped someone would tell him where Benjamin was because he needed to confide in him about something delicate.

Regardless, he made it to Giannis's tent and slipped inside.

Chapter 25

Emerging from the portal, I had no idea where we were. I couldn't even guess which hemisphere we were in. Would they even tell me? I decided to find out.

'You want to tell me where we are?' I asked all four of them.

Before we left, Beelzebub took a moment to introduce his generals. Like all the other demons and angels I'd met so far, they each had one name only. Martha, the female demon, then Aksel, Bitrius, and Acadus. They each looked at me but getting introduced, none of them offered to shake my hand or even nodded their head in my direction as a form of greeting.

'Anastasia is a great asset to us. You will protect her at all costs,' said Beelzebub before we left his chambers. I thought they were trying to kill me in Osaka, and maybe they were, but their orders now were to take me wherever I needed to go and help me retrieve the remaining pieces of armour. Like Daniel, they could not enter any of the religious buildings we were going to visit so their usefulness was limited unless

I ran into trouble, but given how many people they killed in Japan, I doubted I wanted to have them rescue me.

I was stuck in a difficult position, needing to find a way to spoil Beelzebub's plan, but also needing to give him what he wanted just to stay alive long enough to have a chance to find a way to effect a change.

Martha turned her head and eyes to look down at me. 'How did you know to look in New York and Osaka?' she demanded to know.

'I'm really clever,' I growled back, not liking her attitude.

She stiffened at my insult and started to raise her sword. Acadus stepped in to block her. 'There can be none of that, Martha. Beelzebub made it quite clear we are to are tolerate her as we obtain the armour.' He held her gaze for a second before looking my way. 'We are in Mostar in what the humans now call Bosnia. We have reason to believe a piece of the armour is here.'

I frowned slightly. 'Reason to believe? What reason?'

'Research has been conducted. Using familiars to look for the markers, we have been able to find three sites, one of which, the temple in Osaka, you already raided.' Acadus was speaking to me as an equal though I felt sure he didn't consider me to be one. He, at least, didn't make me want to instantly kill him, though I still planned to if the chance arose. 'Another site was this one. There were reports a few months ago of a shifter wielding the shield. The reports must be false since no mortal can wear the armour, but the demon who provided the report then vanished and hasn't been seen since. He was not the only one to go missing here.' Acadus led me to a corner where before me suddenly was an enormous church. 'This is the cathedral of the Parish of Mary Mother of the Church. That's a direct translation, of course. It sounds more elegant in the native tongue.'

It was showtime, whether I liked it or not, but before I could get my mental state into gear and start toward the church, I got a hard shove from behind to get me moving.

I spun about, 'Hey!'

It was Martha staring down at me again, willing me to start something she wanted to finish. She would get her chance, I felt certain of that, but now was not the right time. She snarled at me, 'Get moving.' I shot her an amused smile, which angered her yet more, and I turned my back on her to show how uninteresting she was to me. When she shoved me again, I was ready.

The heel of her palm jolted my right shoulder, just as it had the previous time, but on this occasion, I spun around, changing direction and swinging off my back foot as I drew source energy into my right hand. I was already most of a foot shorter than her, and as I spun, I dropped, so when I thrust out my right hand there wasn't a thing she could do to stop me and I caught her completely by surprise.

I released the sinfire at the exact moment my hand touched her left knee and got to watch with glee as the energy propelled her leg back up the street we were coming out of. It was as if her foot were tied to a car that had suddenly driven in the other direction. She let out a small yelp, but it was silenced when her face hit the road.

Hands were grabbing my shoulders and dragging me away, the three male demons deciding it would be best to get me inside the cathedral now. They would deal with Martha.

Acadus and Aksel led me to the old building but stopped fifty yards short. 'Go now,' ordered Aksel. 'Retrieve whatever is inside and be quick about it.'

I had a dozen different snarky replies lined up, but I didn't bother to use any of them. I was clinging to something Daniel had said and hoping I could not only prove it to be true but turn it to my advantage. He said there might be more weapons and now the sword was in Beelzebub's hand, I really had to hope he was right.

The cathedral sat in a town square which looked the sort to be filled with tourists sitting around tables and chairs as they ate and drank from restaurants dotted around the periphery. One building had a clock high on its front façade. It showed the time to be twelve fifteen in the morning which is why the square was currently devoid of any life. I had no idea what day it was and doubted I could even work it out if I tried. It hardly mattered.

A few days ago, I had broken into Rochester cathedral in England. It was the first time I had ever broken into anywhere and despite already possessing my ability to channel source energy, I had used an old road sign I found to force the lock mechanism on a back door. I wasn't going to mess around with any of that this time.

I strode across the street, pulling source energy in and much like I had with Martha's leg, I rammed the outgoing sinfire into the hinge of the large main door and watched it buckle inward. I gave it a second but the wailing alarm I worried I might hear didn't go off and the cloud of dust coming through the hole I made wasn't as bad as expected.

Tugging my top down and my stupid hipster trousers up again because neither garment felt like it was covering me, I went inside. Using a ball of sinfire in my right hand to chase away the darkness, I started to look about.

I knew from a history class I barely paid attention to that there had been a war in this region a few years before I was born. Back in the early nineties, Croatia, Bosnia, and a few smaller states had ripped each other apart to resolve ancient differences and disputes over borders that had been held in check by Soviet rule for decades. The cathedral looked to have been caught up in that fighting. Even in the dim light emitted from an orb of sinfire in my right hand, I could see where parts of the ceiling looked new and I found bullet marks in the old stonework.

The bullet marks got me excited initially because the first ones I saw, high up above my head, looked like the marker symbol in the poor light and long shadows. However, the additional marks in the stone just made finding what I was looking for harder.

Cursing my forgetfulness, I remembered the trick I'd employed in Osaka and dropped the source energy I held. As I drew in a fresh charge, I waited for the familiar tugging feeling to come.

I kept waiting.

Pursing my lips, I tried again but got the same result. This was annoying and it meant I was going to have to find the marker by the original method of using my eyes. Setting off around the old cathedral with a sinfire ball high above my head, I knew I was at least safe from the demons here, and then it hit me.

I could just wait here until the sun came up in a few hours. The four demons waiting outside would have to flee the sun and ... then what? I would be stuck in Bosnia. That wouldn't be insurmountable, I told myself though I had no idea what I would do to get myself home, I needed someone around who could open portals. Without that, I wasn't a lot of use to anyone.

Before I could give it any further thought, I found the marker. It was high on a round column at the front of the church. I brought my eyes back to face height where I could see the column's outer surface looked different. Extending down to the floor, the column's lower five or so feet looked new. It looked ... it looked to have been replaced and my heart skipped a beat when I guessed what might have happened. The shield, or whatever it was that had been here, had been hidden inside the column however long ago it came to Bosnia, but had been disturbed during the war.

Exposed when the column was damaged, it was clear that whether it had been the shield here or something different, it was gone now. Where was it, though? The answer to that question was the one I needed to know. Hearing Acadus tell me it was the shield had given me a faint inkling of hope – would I be able to use it as a weapon? Could I channel source energy through it and employ it to kill my handlers.

At the time, Beelzebub's warning of eternal torment rang in my ears, but I wasn't going to let that stop me - I'd never been one for obeying threats or orders. It didn't matter now because the shield wasn't here. That was why I didn't get the tugging sensation when I connected to the source.

I took a moment to consider my next move. I was trying to work out how to utilise the information Alex had almost certainly amassed now. There were so many players in this game and, not for the first time, I wondered about what role the SIA might play in the fight to come. I hadn't met them yet and I only knew they were pursuing me from DS Spencer. However, if the Earth were going to unite against the demon threat, I would need help, and the SIA were the closest I could get to people who knew what was going on.

It was time to find out how reasonable the four demons outside could be.

Chapter 26

The SIA

S winton knew it was coming. Ironbolt was a micromanager to an extreme point when it came to matters outside of his home turf and that seemed to apply doubly for Swinton's jurisdiction in the UK.

No phone call this time, he had been summoned to join a video conference so the head of the SIA could see his face. Clicking the button of his mouse with an annoyed jab, he watched as the American's head appeared on his screen.

'Good evening,' Commissioner Swinton started to say, planning to greet his boss formally before they got down to business and switching to American time since it was very early morning in London.

Ironbolt just cut him off. 'What is the status of the situation in New York?' he demanded to know.

Working hard not to react to the man's rudeness, Swinton ran a hand down the length of his tie to make sure it was in place, a nervous habit he wasn't even aware of, then said, 'My agents are waiting for Miss Aaronson to return to the house.'

'Waiting?' barked Ironbolt. 'So they're not doing a damned thing.'

'Those were my instructions.' Swinton was already getting annoyed. 'What use is there in raiding the property if Miss Aaronson is not there?' He intended it as a rhetorical question, but he got an immediate answer.'

'Are you stupid, man? With the target out of the property you can create an ambush for her inside. Not only that, your agents could have taken into protective custody, the persons travelling with Miss Aaronson. That's what I read in the report, isn't it?' Swinton opened his mouth to speak but Ironbolt steamrollered right over him. 'The arresting officer from England,' he looked down at his notes, 'one Detective Sergeant Spencer seems to have gone rogue and a large woman who matches the description of a woman Miss Aaronson works with. That was the house she was spotted at in Rochester.' Ironbolt threw his hands in the air. It was his biggest issue with the British: they never wanted to attack a problem. They were so bookish and studious, always trying to analyse when a good ass-kicking would have got the job done already.

Swinton hadn't considered the strategy his boss was now suggesting. It hadn't even occurred to him to invade the private property of an American citizen and he knew the woman to be the daughter of a senator and her husband to be a New York cop. The SIA were supposed to be a clandestine organisation. Raiding properties on foreign soil was a good way to get noticed. Hadn't Ironbolt thought of that?

'I'm taking over,' snapped the American.

All Swinton could manage in response was, 'What?'

'You heard me. I can't have this bungled any longer. I will have my agents liaise with your men and include them in the raid. There can be no more sitting about. You are to cease all contact with your agents. Don't even answer them if they call you.'

'Sir, I don't think you have considered the full potential of what you are suggesting,'

Ironbolt cut him off again. 'Have you heard anything from the wizard?'

Swinton knew his boss meant Otto Schneider even though they were tracking several known supernaturals with elemental magical power. Disappointingly, he had to admit, 'No, sir. No response at all. His last communication was more than a week ago and he was still tracking familiars.'

Ironbolt sighed. 'You don't know where he is either? Do you know anything?' Ironbolt knew he was being unfair now, but he didn't care. The British head of the SIA was the wrong man for the job and needed to be replaced by someone more competent. That was a task he would attend to shortly. First, he wanted to tell his own boss they were making progress. There was rumour of a weapon – a sword – from several eyewitness reports taken at the scene of a skirmish in Rochester three nights ago. Then he had a cathedral raided in New York last night and, apparently, there was a battle in Osaka, Japan just a few hours ago. The report he read placed the attack right outside of an ancient temple. Something was occurring and it was his job to find out what that was.

Ayla Pendragon had rights, but he was about to overrule them for the good of his nation and the world. Her father was a patriot; a man who fought in the first Iraq war, leading an Infantry Regiment into battle. Perhaps his daughter would prove to be the same and would cooperate.

His men would be going into an environment where the threat level was unknown so it would be maximum penetration until the civilians inside were secure. It should have been conducted during daylight, and Ironbolt blamed himself for not tackling this earlier. A daylight raid would have nullified the chance of finding a demon inside the house. Too late now, he wasn't prepared to wait until morning.

He dismissed Swinton, ended the call, and picked up his phone to summon his head of operations. It was time to kick some butt.

Chapter 27

Emerging from the cathedral in Mostar, I discovered the four demons were nowhere in sight. They soon emerged from shadows across the street, appearing spread out across a hundred yards or more – a sensible tactic for not being seen and being able to respond if one were attacked.

I waited for them to come to me, and it made me smile when they all stopped fifty yards shy of the church.

'Where is the artefact?' demanded Bitrius.

'Already gone,' I called back to him. They were surrounding me and still spread out like I was the batsman and they were the basemen.

'She's lying,' replied Martha in what I was already coming to think of as typical Martha fashion.

I narrowed my eyes at her. 'Go check for yourself.' Instantly, she had hellfire in her hands. I spread my arms and welcomed her. 'Go on, girl. Take your best shot. I bet you can't even hit me.' I goaded her because

I wanted the hellfire to power me up. A little extra zing stored inside would not hurt when my opportunity came.

Aksel ignored the interplay. 'How can you be sure it is gone?' he asked.

Martha wasn't going to hit me with hellfire, more's the pity, so I turned my attention to answer his question. 'Through the pieces of armour I have, I can feel when other pieces are near. There is nothing in the cathedral. The marker is located above a column that had been repaired. You told me you knew of it because a demon saw it here – maybe they really did and there is another like me who was able to retrieve it.'

My suggestion drew them into a huddle. They didn't like that idea, not one bit. Before they could get into it, a set of headlights began to illuminate one of the streets which led into the square and the sound of a car approaching heralded the arrival of a police patrol car. Mostly likely, it was on a routine patrol, but it paused when it saw the five of us in front of the cathedral. I doubted they could see the damage to the door, but when they shone a spotlight our way, I knew it was going to go bad if we didn't get out of here.

'You need to take me to the next place,' I insisted.

The police employed their loudspeaker to say something. It was in Croatian though so I didn't understand it. Acadus formed a ball of hellfire and he would have destroyed their squad car had I not stepped up and grabbed his arm.

He flinched, automatically trying to snatch his arm away though I held it tightly. 'To New York,' I begged. 'Take me there. I have friends working to identify other likely places where we can find the pieces of armour.'

He yanked his arm free. 'Don't touch me, mortal,' and I thought he was going to kill the cops just to prove a point. Aksel, however, had opened a portal and was waiting to go through. I raised my right hand to him, letting the flesh to flesh contact draw me from one realm to the next.

Chapter 28

Daniel found himself mired with indecision. Whatever course he took, the result seemed likely to end in disaster. However, his cycle of considering options and discarding them had led him back to his need to rescue Anastasia. Whether he then used her to get the armour and betrayed her to present Beelzebub with a gift that might allow Daniel to return to some form of standing in the ruler's court, or chose instead to betray the demons and side with Anastasia and the humans was something he could decide later. He leaned heavily toward the former of the two choices because the humans were going to lose even if Anastasia did prove herself to be invincible with the sword and armour.

It was in his indecision that his opportunity arose. Beelzebub's grand house lay ahead of him. He had been there many times to present familiars to his leader; the enormous house required a great number of servants to keep it in good shape. Watching it for hours as he tried to come up with a way that he, with no support, could get in, find Anastasia and get out, he saw something else instead and it was much sweeter than he could have hoped for.

It was a raiding party of angels.

He saw Benjamin when he came through a portal two hundred yards away. At that distance, he was hard to make out, and it was only because he recognised the same clothes the angel wore for the battle in Osaka that he felt confident it was him.

There were hundreds of angels materialising across a wide swathe of land. All the demons – well, almost all – lived in this area but the nature of Beelzebub's abode meant none of them were within a mile of it. It was surrounded by open countryside which made an attack like this possible.

Even so, Daniel couldn't deny his surprise that Godfrey would commit to such a bold tactic. Maybe he felt they had no choice. Benjamin must have reported that the demons had Anastasia and therefore also the sword. With the armour too, Beelzebub became effectively unstoppable and Godfrey's grand scheme to prevent it ever falling into his brother's hands was undone.

This was going to be a lightning raid, that much Daniel guessed; the angels would need to get in and out again before the demons could respond and there would be demons inside the grand house they would have to get through to obtain their target.

Acting quickly to seize his unexpected chance, Daniel levered himself off the rock he'd spent the last few hours resting on and started after the angels. They were ahead of him, but he was willing to bet none of them knew the layout of Beelzebub's house – that was why they opened portals in the grounds outside and not directly into the house.

He could let them clear the way, go around the fighting and get to Anastasia first. He had a fairly good idea where she was. Though he had only been there once, Beelzebub had a punishment room in his basement he called 'the pit'. Demons who displeased him had been known to go in there and not be seen for weeks or months as they were endlessly tortured.

He was destined to go there when Anastasia killed Nathaniel and he managed to escape with her. That he was going to make his own way there now defied logic and all good sense. If he got caught, his existence would become a misery he refused to imagine. To get to Anastasia he had no choice.

Sooner than he expected, the first trade of sinfire and hellfire filled the quiet trees with noise.

Chapter 29

DS Spencer knew it wasn't cold enough out for it to do him any harm, but he was getting really cold now. It had seeped into his core and up through the soles of his shoes to make the bones in his feet ache. Regardless, he continued to watch. Something was happening now.

The trip to the gas station had been nothing more than that, but he was close enough to the man he followed inside to hear his voice when he spoke.

He was English.

Why was the house being watched by two English guys? Not that he could be certain the other fellow was also from Blighty, but it felt like a safe assumption. So too did the guess that they were SIA. Who else would be tailing them? Or even have any interest? Unless Miss Aaronson, wanted for murder and in relation to terrorist activities, had been spotted by CCTV in the streets of Manhattan. Could a neighbour have also seen her? They had been outside the house briefly when they arrived.

It felt like a stretch. Until he remembered something about a wizard and Ayla Pendragon and Miss Aaronson both being connected to him. Was Ayla the one whose image had been spotted and they were outside her house because of that?

All these things had gone around in his head for the last few hours as the sun fell, and he got both cold and hungry. Awhile back, he sent Alex, the oversized librarian, a message to let the people inside the house know that he hadn't been grabbed or anything. He told her he was watching the men watching Ayla's house from a better position and left it at that.

Officer Clint Pendragon, a man DS Spencer could approve of because he was a fellow law enforcement officer, had confirmed, to the best of his ability, that no law enforcement agency was watching his house. When DS Spencer first spotted them, Clint wanted to act, but that would tip their hand and the group discussion managed to dissuade him from leaving the house.

Now, several hours after following the one man to the gas station, they were both sitting in their car when another man approached them. DS Spencer wasn't close enough to hear what was said, but a police officer's nose told him something new had developed. The man crouching at the side of the car to speak through the passenger's window looked like a man with a purpose. He looked ex-military, but that was just one small clue. The bigger tip that something was occurring, was that the two men didn't react. They had been outside

Ayla's house all day without anyone coming near them, and they were English, so unlikely to know anyone here in New York. Now there was this new guy and they didn't seem bothered by their cover being blown.

When the man straightened again, he walked back the way he had come so he hadn't been going somewhere and stopped for a chat; he came to their car purposefully. DS Spencer shivered for the thousandth time and watched the man depart. What did his presence mean? His right foot twitched, once, twice, then he set off after the man to see where he had come from and where he might be going. He abandoned the English chaps because, whether SIA or not, they didn't look likely to be doing anything interesting any time soon.

Five minutes later, he was speed walking back to Ayla Pendragon's house as fast as he could. He wanted desperately to get warm, but it was no longer his most pressing need.

Clint opened the door to find out why someone was hammering on it and had to jump back when DS Spencer shoved his way inside.

'We have to get your family out of here!' he blurted.

The hammering and his outburst drew everyone in the house to the front lobby where DS Spencer was wheezing from walking fast after nearly forty years of smoking too much.

'What is it?' asked Ayla, looking at the prematurely aged man bent double by the front door.

He gasped in a breath. 'I think we might be about to get raided.' He had to pause to get another breath. 'There are more than just the two fellas across the street, who are English, by the way. I think they might be SIA, but whatever they are, there are more guys around the corner. I couldn't get close without giving myself away, but I saw what looked like a tactical van, the kind they use to support ops and control them.'

Alex's hands flew to her face. 'Oh, my God!'

Clint shook his head. 'They wouldn't dare. They can knock on the door if they have a warrant to enter the premises, but they won't just kick the door in.'

Ayla shook her head too. 'I'm not so sure. I met a few of these guys in Germany. They know more than they are letting on and Otto said they have branches everywhere. If they are after Anastasia, then who's to say what they might do.'

Clint looked at his wife. 'I'll get the kids.'

Ayla had her phone out, urgently stabbing the call button. 'Dammit, Otto, where are you?'

Chapter 30

The portal opened back into Beelzebub's house. Stepping through, I found myself looking at the same lush marble floor I had seen before though the room we arrived in was new. Previously, when I travelled with Daniel in the last few days, and, in fact, when he first lured me to go with him, I always arrived in the immortal realm in the middle of nowhere. Coming through from a wide, open town square to find myself inside a well-lit and ornately decorated room threw me for just a moment.

I didn't get time to dwell on it because the hand holding mine didn't let go. The next portal opened as, without any exchange of words, Bitrius conjured one just as Aksel's closed and we were going to New York.

Only the skyline I expected to see with skyscrapers reaching into the night sky was far removed from what lay before me. 'Where is this?' I asked.

Bitrius answered, 'The humans call it Budapest. It's still daylight in New York. We'll go there later.' I hadn't spent long in Mostar – I guessed the time wasn't yet twelve thirty in the morning so it would be hours before the sun came up. My musings about the time were interrupted by Bitrius asking me a question. 'If you can feel when the armour is near another piece, tell me can you sense one near now?'

'Why are we here?' Martha wanted to know.

Bitrius shrugged. 'Just a hunch. The humans have lots of prominent churches, temples, and other historic buildings. I know this to be the largest Jewish place of worship in Europe.'

Acadus snorted a chuckle. 'Humans and their religions. Such an odd concept.'

'I think it's a good thing,' Martha commented. 'Their religions all came from ancient memories of us. They are used to worshipping us as gods. It will help them when the time comes. I intend to be worshipped daily.'

'And if they don't,' I wanted to know.

She fixed me with hard eyes. 'They will know what pain is. I will have a large territory and the humans in it will have the opportunity to prosper provided they honour me. Any who choose not to, choose pain and death.'

I didn't say anything else. I believe that she planned to do exactly as she said and only by stopping her could that fate be changed. That a subjugated people will always rise against their oppressors eventually wasn't a lesson the demons had ever needed to learn. The humans once lived in harmony with the magical race, but the demons' belief the world could return to that state was flawed.

'You want to kill me don't you, little human?' Martha asked it as a question, but it was a statement.

I smiled at her. 'Yes. It's something I plan to do the very first chance I get.'

She tipped back her head and laughed, the male demons all smiling at my audacity. 'How do you propose to do that, little human?' Martha wanted me to explain. 'You no longer have the sword. You cannot do anything to me, whereas I,' she moved her right hand suddenly, but she wasn't trying to hit me, not physically anyway. She had a spell held ready and she hit me with it now, a focused lance of wind striking my midriff to knock the air from my lungs.

When I inevitably doubled over from the unexpected blow, she grabbed my hair and twisted cruelly. 'How would you like another scar to go with the one you have?' she asked, a blade appearing in her free hand so close to my right eye I couldn't focus on it.

'That's enough now, Martha,' chided Aksel. 'We have a task to perform. You can kill her only if Beelzebub allows it.'

'She doesn't need both eyes,' raged the female demon. I think she genuinely meant to do it, and when Aksel grabbed her arm to prevent her from slicing my face open, the blade cut the soft skin under my eye.

When her grip loosened and I got to dance a few steps away, I could already feel the blood running down my face.

I wanted to ask one of them to use source energy to heal the wound but wouldn't dare give them the satisfaction of saying no.

Instead, I walked across to the synagogue and drew in source energy. The tug from the armour was there again. 'There is a piece here,' I announced.

Chapter 31

In Beelzebub's house, the angels were running riot. Giannis had much sway in their community and support for him grew exponentially in the hours after Godfrey attacked him. More than five hundred had assembled in secret to make the raid on the demon stronghold. Any less than that would have been too few but even so, they still needed to move fast for word would get out and more demons would come.

Getting into the house was simplicity itself. In the immortal realm, no one bothers to place guards, so they broke cover and ran for the doors, charging into the house and taking out any demons they found along the way. Their numbers guaranteed overwhelming firepower which beat each demon they discovered into submission very quickly. Then, to prevent their recovery, they bound and gagged them – they didn't want to fight people twice.

Benjamin chose to lead one group, running through the unfamiliar house as he tried to find where they might have the human girl stashed.

The sword was his primary objective, but the girl was important too. Her ability to find the armour and other relics might yet prove pivotal.

They were renegades, he knew that, and he accepted that there would be a reckoning when they returned to the angels' camp. It was already too late to avoid the coming confrontation with Godfrey, but it would be easier to claim righteousness if they returned with the sword and Anastasia Aaronson.

A blast of hellfire, caught him off guard, knocking him off his feet, but the angels to his left and right, and those behind too, swarmed around and over him to deal with the menace. A hand grabbed his and helped him to his feet. It was Gabriel's son, Samuel, who had joined their number without question though he insisted his father could not be trusted to keep it from Godfrey.

'It feels good to be the aggressor,' Samuel laughed, his eyes alive with the potency of battle.

Back on his feet, Benjamin pressed on. 'We have no time to delay,' he insisted as he ran to catch those now forging ahead. 'This place is a maze of a passages to search and more demons will soon come.'

That the word would get out was inevitable. If one demon escaped the house, they would return with a horde too great to overcome, but that wasn't their biggest threat. What worried Benjamin most was the high probability that they would find the sword and it would be held in Beelzebub's giant right hand. How many of their number would he kill? Benjamin was ready to sacrifice himself if it meant others could overpower the demons' leader and regain the sword. With it they could kill Beelzebub and the war against the demons could be over before the death curse fell.

It sounded like too much to hope for, and they had to find him first.

Twenty yards behind Benjamin's group, one of sixteen to break off to search the house, Daniel moved quietly. He stepped over a demon who had been flattened by the angels but was already recovered from the pounding they dished out. The demon, a low caste warrior called Rodrigo looked up at him with expectation. He expected Daniel to set him free and that created a new dilemma. If he did, he then had demons that might get in his way or expect him to join the fight to eject the angels. But if he didn't, it would be recorded not only that he didn't help, but that he was there with the angels.

When he hesitated, Rodrigo started making noises behind his gag. He was getting angry that Daniel wasn't already dealing with the bonds. Seeing no option, Daniel knelt to begin untying the knots.

Before Rodrigo could speak, he whispered, 'Go for help. Bring as many as you can.'

'What are you doing here,' Rodrigo wanted to know. 'I heard you were outcast. I saw you at Beelzebub's feet right before Nathaniel was killed.'

'Secret mission,' Daniel lied, thinking he could probably fool the demon. 'Beelzebub anticipated an attack and wanted me to appear to be turning sides. I infiltrated the angels but wasn't able to broach their inner circle in time to prevent this. Get help. Do it quickly, and we may eliminate a great many of our enemies today.' For added emphasis, he helped Rodrigo to his feet and slapped him on the back. 'I am going to do my best to corral them into Beelzebub's main hall. There we can surround and destroy them.'

Daniel had no idea where the angels were heading but it wasn't in the direction of the main hall. It didn't matter because the moment he got rid of Rodrigo, Daniel was going directly to where he believed Anastasia would be held.

Way ahead of them now, Benjamin's group had run into another team of angels as they all raced forward. How much of the house had they already covered?

When they then chanced upon Giannis, they had to pause to discuss what they had achieved.

'I've found nothing but demons so far,' complained Giannis.

'There has to be areas we haven't seen yet,' said Ursula, the raven-haired angel leading a third group. When they heard footsteps running toward them, almost a hundred angels swung their hands to repel whoever was coming but bursting from a side passage was yet another group of angels.

They looked panicked and breathless and the passageway behind them was filled with flashes of both light blue and dark red light as those behind the angels Benjamin could now see fought whoever was giving chase.

'It's Beelzebub!' screamed a young male angel called Christopher. 'He just killed Antonia and Julius!'

Ursula instantly began to open a portal. 'We must escape!' she shouted so all would hear and know to flee.

Benjamin grabbed her arm to stop her. 'No!' His bellow echoed off the walls. 'We have to stop him now. If we fail, he will only get stronger. Did you really think we would all get out of this alive?'

Giannis agreed with him. 'We have to fight now. Regardless of the odds. If we can overpower him before his reinforcements arrive, we can win this day and end his reign before it begins. If we let him get the armour too, none will be able to stand against him.'

Chapter 32

Colt Ironbolt was going to arrive in New York in just a few minutes, his helicopter from the roof of the SIA headquarters in DC took just ninety minutes to cover the distance and was a perfect way to demonstrate how the money budgeted to them ought to be spent. He didn't want this team to wait for his arrival though, much preferring to have plausible deniability for any problems that might arise by not being there.

He was, however, the one required to give the word to go.

Talking to his tactical commander on the ground, he wet his lips, savouring the moment because it was one of those days when he could feel he was going to come out looking every bit the hero. Not only that, his agents loved that he gave them autonomy to perform tasks such as this one in the way they deemed.

After holding his breath for a two count, he said a single word, 'Go,' then relaxed back into his seat in the back of the bird. Looking at the lights of late evening New York now filling the front glass of the helicopter's cockpit, he visualised the activity springing into action in a quiet New York suburb. It would be over by the time he got there, but that just meant he could put the next part into play: the capture of Anastasia Aaronson. How hard could one small woman be to take into custody? She was either a terrorist with supernatural powers in which case he intended to have her quietly killed, or she was a being of great importance, and if that was the case, he needed to recruit her.

Feeling supremely confident, he closed his eyes and let his mind drift. He would be there shortly.

In Ayla's house, Clint was calling cop buddies to get cars rolling his way, Anton was fretting again and Ayla was doing her best to be happy positive mom to her two small children who were now out of bed way past their bedtime and very confused about what was going on.

Alex said, 'The two guys in the car across the street just moved. It looks like ... they are, they are getting out of their car. What does that mean?' Her question was directed more toward DS Spencer than anyone else and he answered because he was closest and because he had an answer.

'It means this is happening now.'

Across the street, Garfield and Riddle were high on adrenalin. The American SIA agent, a man called Warner Stubbs, wanted them to walk up to the door and knock on it. It was a respect thing, Warner told them, because this was their stakeout. In truth, Warner's commander knew how Ironbolt thought and agreed with his policy of having scapegoats. If this all went south and someone, an innocent, got hurt, then it was the British agents who moved first. It would be claimed they were acting without orders when they approached the house and the US agents had to bail them out. The whole thing became a tragic fiasco because of the British. Of course, if it all went well, then they could claim a spirit of mutual cooperation and inclusion – yessir, we had the British agents play a key role in apprehending the dangerous supernaturals.

Garfield and Riddle just weren't paranoid enough to question what Agent Stubbs told them. Their inclusion felt natural and though they knew they were only getting a small role, their mission had been to find and bring Anastasia Aaronson home. With a little help from the local boys, they might just pull it off. It's the result that counts, right? Teamwork, Warner had reminded them, was vital to defeating any problem.

'You or me?' asked Riddle.

Garfield cut his eyes to the side as they started up the front lawn. 'You or me what?'

'To knock on the door. It only needs one of us. You can do it if you like. I don't mind either way.'

Garfield raised one eyebrow; his partner was seriously discussing who should knock on the door like it was a prestigious honour or something. Skipping to the end of the conversation, he said, 'You knock, and I'll talk to them.' They had one shot at speaking to the people inside. Warner's instructions were to identify themselves and request the people inside the house surrender to the SIA. They would not be incarcerated, but their involvement with Anastasia Aaronson demanded they be questioned at a private facility. Riddle and Garfield were to convince them this was the wise option to take, since the alternative was to be taken by force.

Of course, Warner then planned to put SIA operatives inside the house so they could capture Aaronson when she returned and that was the bit the British agents were interested in.

Garfield had a whole speech lined up in his head. He needed to get the message across quickly and get a fast response. Nothing else was acceptable, Warner assured him. He was going to have sixty seconds from the time the door opened. If he hadn't confirmed their peaceful surrender by then, the SIA would enter by force.

The British agents never made it to the door.

When they were halfway across the dark lawn, a light above the door flicked on and the door opened. Framed in the light was a pissed off looking cop, in full uniform, with his badge showing and his gun raised three quarters of the way. Just to his left was Ayla Pendragon, who they recognised because they had a file on her. Her hair was beginning to float, a sure sign she was sucking in a ton of ley line energy, and that meant she had a spell waiting to go.

The appearance of the homeowners in such a threatening display caught the two shifters off guard. They were tough because of their supernatural nature, but in general terms, a werewolf can only challenge a wizard once transformed. They also weren't bulletproof.

Their instant reaction was to begin the transformation, it happened almost automatically upon feeling threatened for all shifters and then had to be fought if they didn't want to change.

Yet again, they didn't get a chance to consider it either way because six cop cars screeched around the corner and into the road from two different directions and hit their sirens just as they came into view.

'This is private property,' shouted Clint Pendragon, taking the first step down off his stoop. 'Interlace your fingers and place them behind your heads.'

The cop cars sped closer, braking late to pull up at the last second. The men and women inside had received a call from one of their own and they were ready to do violence if necessary: No one threatens a cop in New York and gets away with it.

A hundred and fifty yards away around the corner, in a trailer filled with electronic wizardry, the on-scene commander sucked on his teeth. He was ex-military and well used to intricate plans going out the window six seconds into the battle. This time, though, he had expected a smooth result. Viewing the events from a camera slung under a drone, he saw the peaceful, easy solution go south. It was out of control and now his problem to recover.

'Rear team, enter the property now. I want all the civilians inside in custody.' The order would be acted upon instantly, he knew that much. However, the cops at the front of the property were going to be a problem and he needed to deal with it in person. 'Front team, make yourself visible. Show your weapons but do not act aggressively.

Show identification when the officers demand it. I am on route to you now.' Then to his driver, he said, 'Let's roll.' It would take ten seconds to get there and this would be over ten seconds after that. He had jurisdiction, but the cops weren't going to go away easily and that was the biggest problem.

Or so he thought. He was very badly wrong.

Standing on his doorstep, Officer Clint Pendragon felt genuinely good. Two men had been staking out his house which had been an affront to him all day, but he had handled it. With the help from a few friends admittedly, but that was what being a cop was all about. He was going to arrest them himself, but halfway to them, things went sideways.

Both men, who had been obediently holding their hands behind their heads, grabbed the back of their collars and ripped off all the clothes on their top half in one go. The move elicited shouts from every officer converging on them, but the very sudden appearance of three dozen armed men in black combat fatigues kind of caused a distraction.

They seemed to come from everywhere. That was Ayla's impression as they materialised from behind trees, around the side of houses and out from behind Mrs Grosvenor's hedge across the street.

She had lightning primed in her hand and was ready to throw it, but the lawn was littered with both good guys and bad and she wasn't accurate enough to hit one and not the other.

The cops were shouting for the guys in black to drop their weapons and for the two half naked men to lie down, but too many things were happening at once, not least of which was the two topless men transforming before her eyes. She knew werewolves were real just from talking to Otto and other familiars, but this was the first time she'd ever seen one.

The men in their black combat outfits had their hands off their weapons and they were talking in calm tones. Behind them in the street, a large matt-grey truck pulled to a stop, but her attention was drawn to a crashing noise behind her as the rear team invaded her house.

Just exiting the rear of the truck, the on-scene commander, a veteran of more than thirty years' service with the military and the SIA by the name of Chuck 'Charles' Houston, was listening to the chatter over the radio. It was all happening as he wanted. His agents at the front of the house had tied up the cops long enough for the agents at the rear to safely infiltrate. It wasn't the clean take he originally planned, but it would do.

Almost no one saw the portal opening in the neighbour's driveway. Ayla had ducked back inside her house and was running to see what the crashing noise was. In her right hand was an air spell that was going to wreck her kitchen. She was pissed about the damage about to be wrought, but far too angry to stop. Chuck Houston didn't see the portal open because he was looking the wrong way and raising his hands to get the attention of everyone present. In fact, the only ones who saw the figure emerge from the portal were Garfield and Riddle, who were now fully transformed and desperate to shed their trousers and shoes, and Officer Cindy Lee, a short Chinese cop on her third month as a probationary officer. The gum fell out of her mouth.

Chapter 33

Otto Schneider arrived with a spell poised on his fingers and bad attitude on his breath. He didn't miss the first message from Ayla, he simply hadn't been in a position to respond to it. The news channel showed grainy footage of her fighting a demon and told him it was by a cathedral in Manhattan. The fact that he got the message from her after it occurred, told him she was alive and okay and that had stalled his desire to run to her aide. The second message made him drop everything. She only sent him three words.

'I need you.'

His eyes took in multiple targets, most of them human, and unable to see Ayla, he started flinging magic around. Between the shifters, the cops, and whoever the heck the guys in black were, he had plenty of targets. The cops seemed to have the upper hand; certainly, they were the ones with their guns raised, but when Otto realised he couldn't see any innocents in any direction, he flicked his left hand and let the air spell he held rip.

He opened the portal expecting to find Ayla in trouble on the other side, but she wasn't in sight. It was her house he was looking at and she had close to fifty people crowding her front lawn and sidewalk. The power of Otto's spell took them all down in one hit, Ayla's husband included though Otto didn't recognise him at the time. A wave of air went across the ground at a height of about six inches which was like triggering a giant tripwire. It took out the feet of everyone in sight and once they were down, Otto pulled in moisture, agitating the molecules to create static electricity which he held ready as he stalked forward.

One of the cops was the first to swing his weapon in the German wizard's direction, his reward a bolt of controlled lightning that worked just like a taser being fired. Everyone saw what he did, and before Otto could knock more of them out, a lone member of the SIA strike squad fired his weapon.

The short burst of five rounds from his assault rifle had crossed the ground between him and Otto before anyone heard the sound, but the rounds impacted on Otto's defensive shield, an invisible wall of energy which had saved his life more times than he could count.

Bored with wondering what might be going on, Otto sent a lightning bolt at the black-clad gunman and shouted, 'Ayla!' as loud as he could manage.

In the kitchen, the pots and pans were still in the air when Otto started flinging lightning at people, but in such a contained space, the energy of Ayla's spell proved too much for the windows and the back door, popping them from their frames just before the loose items her spell collected went through them. It all flew from the back of the house into her yard with a deafening cacophony of noise.

It was certainly enough to draw Otto's attention, yet he had only enough time to start moving in that direction before a spark of light to his right drew his eye and his stomach clenched with the latest problem.

A portal was opening.

Otto knew he was the only mortal ever to work out how to conjure a portal for himself, which meant what was coming through was most likely a demon. At best case, it was going to be shilt arriving and he could see them off with a flick of his wrist.

It wasn't shilt though. He recognised the four characters emerging from the bright portal: they were Beelzebub's generals and therefore some of the most powerful and deadliest demons he could face. But even as he bared his teeth and began to pull ley line energy in to fuel his coming onslaught of spells, he saw a fifth person run ahead of them.

What the heck was Anastasia Aaronson doing with Beelzebub's generals? There were more questions besides, like why or even how was it that she appeared to have pieces of armour floating above her skin? There was no time to ask them though for the demons had all seen the mass of humans before them and were charging their hands with hellfire.

Otto let them have everything he held, raining lightning down onto them without mercy the moment he thought he could do so without hitting Anastasia.

Chapter 34

My foray into the synagogue had been more successful, but only in so far as there had been something, rather than nothing, there for me to find. It was a piece of armour that went on my forearm and was already floating above my skin before I left the building to rejoin the demons outside.

It wasn't so much that I wanted to go to New York, but more that I had been missing for a day already, had no idea what might have happened to Daniel, and most of all, if I wanted to find any more of the pieces, I needed to know what Alex might have dug up.

Acadus bounced us in the immortal realm and out again so briefly that they got to see the fight taking place in Beelzebub's house only as the portal was closing once more and we were on our way to New York.

'There are angels in Beelzebub's house!' raged Bitrius, his words like venom. They were going back, but if I could get away just as they opened the portal to return, I could see my friends, get them safe, and wait for the demons to return for me.

'We're going back!' shouted Aksel, getting ready to open a fresh portal even as we stepped through the one to New York. The air temperature dropped and the moment we materialised in the mortal realm, I yanked my hand free and dove out of the way.

It was only when I was throwing myself clear of the demons and expecting them to vanish behind me that I became aware of the fight raging here too. There were dozens of people on the grass outside of Ayla's house. Cops, guys with assault rifles dressed like a tactical unit, and right across from me, none other than Otto Schneider, a man I had a bunch of questions to ask.

Still moving away from the demons and their portal, I heard their shouts change as they too saw the scene before them. I don't know if they saw Otto Schneider and recognised him, or if the armed mortals swung weapons their way, but I could feel the source energy getting drawn in their direction. I sucked in some of my own, drawing it into my body to fuel my own weapon, but as I did, I felt my hair lift, and in that moment, folded my legs and dove for the ground.

The world became a blinding flash of intensely bright light that seared my eyes even with them tightly shut. Blinking a second later, huge coronas remained to blur my vision. With source energy inside my body, I charged my right hand with sinfire and tried to get up.

The immense discharge of electrical power had messed with my head. Even though it hadn't touched me, the fading light in my eyes had thrown off my balance and there was no time for that. I could die if I failed to move.

'Otto!' I screamed his name. We didn't know each other, not really. He'd saved me from harm at the hands of another wizard, but only as a courtesy. He was there to stop the wizard, not prevent my death. He'd come back to help me afterward though and taught me a few things I didn't know before running out to save someone called Heike when I needed him most. I'd survived, so who was to say whether his decision to abandon me was right or wrong. Either way, I wanted his help now.

My vision was coming back which meant I could see the demons getting back to their feet behind me. The cops and the tactical team – were they on the same side? – were angry like a swarm of buzzing bees and before I could stop them, someone gave the order to open fire.

Bullets ripped through the air as the world erupted into deafening sound which assaulted a second of my senses in a manner that threatened to overload it. I was used to hearing weapons being fired, but usually wore ear defence because the constant noise could make a person deaf quite quickly.

The aiming point was the demons, who having recovered from the unexpected lightning assault, were now getting to their feet, and forming hellfire. Bullets tore into them, but they launched their hellfire assault anyway.

It had a devastating effect.

Bodies of cops and tactical agents tumbled to the ground whenever a trace of hellfire touched them. With a scream, I sent a stream of sinfire right into the demons. The sustained blast of source energy proved too much as I felt certain it would, stopping all four from killing anyone else, but it also drew the attention of the armed men and women behind me to the, thus far, unnoticed smallest player on the field.

I had no defence against bullets as demonstrated when I got shot less than twenty-four hours ago.

The first rounds hit my breastplate, lifting me off the ground and driving all the air from my lungs. Flying backward I remarked to myself on the accuracy of the shooter's grouping, the volley of rounds all hitting the intended target centre of mass in a tight circle.

Of course, now I was down, my efforts were not keeping the demons from getting up which is what they did, firing orb upon orb into the press of human targets.

I really needed a moment to recover – getting shot, even when wearing magical armour, is still like getting hit with a sledgehammer. There wasn't time for me to take a break though; people were dying while I struggled for breath. From the grass, I drew in more source energy; I had to stop the demons from hurting anyone else. If I didn't diffuse this situation, they might kill everyone, including me if Martha got a chance.

Otto wasn't done either. Not by half. Just as I pulled myself around to line up and fire a fresh stream (terrified I was about to get shot by a human again), the demons' onslaught of deadly hellfire abruptly stopped. They had barely moved from the spot they were on when they stepped from the portal, but now each was impaled through the chest by a giant icicle. It came downwards through the top of their ribs and out through their backs to bury itself in the ground.

The shouting and screaming from the cops and tactical agents stopped as if someone had shut off a valve. One second people were barking orders and their weapons were firing, then next I thought I would be able to hear birdsong if there were any.

In his rough German accent, Otto said, 'That ought to hold them.'

It would. Just not for very long.

I swung my head around to look at him with startled eyes. The demons are so dismissive of elemental magic but here it was in action, taking out four of them in one go. If they were not immortal, they would be dead.

'Where did you get icicles?' I gasped, hugging myself against the cold and wishing I still had the My Little Pony hoody.

Otto didn't answer me; he was weaving a new spell. I couldn't tell what it was until the cops and tactical guys started yelling and gasping and dropping their weapons. Otto had sent heat to make them too hot to hold, something I knew was possible with elemental magic. Now the humans were disarmed, Otto started to stride forward to look at the demons. On his way, he conjured something new. 'I pulled moisture down from the upper atmosphere,' he explained without bothering to look at me. 'This isn't enough though.'

Just as Otto raised his hands, from behind him, a man yelled, 'Hey! What are you doing? I need them alive.' Otto paid him no attention, pulling in more moisture, and forming it into ice to freeze the four demons in one giant block.

'You are the man in charge?' Otto asked.

'I am Commander Chuck Houston on the SIA. You are Otto Schneider, yes? I need you to step aside now. The demons are now my prisoners as is Miss Aaronson.' He turned his eyes toward me. 'I would rather you came peacefully, Miss Aaronson.'

A reply sprang to my lips but the front door of Ayla's house exploding outward onto the front lawn stopped me from delivering it.

Chapter 35

One of the cops was the first to react. Ayla's husband, I realised, when he screamed her name and ran for the house. Everyone turned in the same direction, all alert to the new danger, but before Clint could make it to the steps leading into the house, Ayla stepped out. She had a line of blood coming from her hairline and another from the right corner of her mouth. From her hands, which trailed at her sides, she had the limp bodies of two more men in tactical gear.

'Honey, we might need to redecorate,' she said with an odd little laugh which did little to mask the rage boiling inside her.

Her hands opened, dropping the two men as she reached the steps, they tumbled down to lie on the ground, and she stepped over them. Clint rushed to her side, wrapping her into a hug but after the briefest of embraces, she moved him aside and continued forward.

'Which of you is in charge?' she demanded.

I noted the flash of nerves passing over Commander Houston's face as eyes swung his way. It was much akin to everyone pointing their fingers.

Appearing in the doorway now were Alex, Anton, DS Spencer, and Ayla's two small children. The kids were being carried by Alex and Anton, their wide eyes showing even though they clung to the adults like limpets to a rock in a storm.

'I am Commander Houston of the SIA and I am in charge here,' stated Houston, filling his chest with confidence as he moved to take centre stage. Ayla twitched her right hand to send a shot of lightning from the floor into his legs.

Houston twitched and keeled over. 'Anyone else want to volunteer to be in charge?' she snarled.

There had to be twenty bodies lying on her lawn, some of them were cops and the people who remained were caught in a confusion of looking out for further danger and trying to give aid to their fallen comrades even though nothing could be done for them.

At Ayla's challenge several of the SIA raised their hands in surrender, but their move was not mirrored by the remaining cops who had to be questioning what the hell was going on and mentally logging this as the weirdest call they ever responded to.

As the argument raged, no one, not even me, was paying attention to the demons encased in their block of ice. Had I been, I might have noticed the tiny spot of dark red beginning to glow inside the ice.

The cops and the SIA agents were all shouting at each other, both sides claiming jurisdiction, but it was clear which side Ayla was going with. 'Otto would you be a sweet and give me a hand. Asphyxiation, I think, yes?'

Wordlessly, Otto nodded his head and I got to see a trick I remembered experiencing first hand when Sean McGuire used it on me. I'd beaten it by blasting him with sinfire, but the SIA agents were not so lucky. Both wizards raised their hands, manipulating the air to shut off the supply to the tactical agents' lungs.

Instantly, eyes bugged out of heads; the SIA agents panicking as the wizards prevented them from drawing breath. Ayla and Otto weren't going to kill them, I felt certain, this was just to subdue them.

The sound of a helicopter approaching reached my ears, but I figured it was more cops as I searched the night sky for it. On Ayla's front lawn, the SIA agents were beginning to drop. There were more of them than there were cops, but in seconds it was over, the supernaturals demonstrating what they could do against superior numbers.

A memory surfaced with a jolt: supernaturals! There had been two shifters here before. I saw them when I first arrived.

I blurted, 'Werewolves!' as I spun on the spot to look for them. Otto and Ayla had both been lowering their hands but they lifted them again as each looked about with wary eyes.

'What's that now?' asked a female cop. 'Did I just hear the crazy white girl say werewolves?'

I ignored her. 'I think they are SIA too,' said DS Spencer. 'I saw them transform from the window. That had got to be some of the craziest shi ...'

'Don't shoot!' begged a voice from the front of the house. 'Or, you know, don't do whatever it is you can do with those hands.'

From underneath the house, where it sat raised a foot off the ground, crawled the two shifters. They were still fully transformed into were-wolves and would have looked scary as all hell if they hadn't looked so scared of us. They had their hands up as they got first to their knees and then slowly to their feet.

'Doggies!' exclaimed the little girl Alex held. Her excited remark broke Ayla's glare, and, as if remembering her children for the first time in minutes, she ran to them.

'We were just sent to find Miss Aaronson,' said the one on the left, nodding his head in my direction while looking at everyone else. His hands were still up when he added. 'We had no idea any of this was going to happen.'

'Are those guys dead?' asked the one next to him as he looked at the inert figures lying all around us.

The noise of the helicopter, which had been getting louder for some time, reached a volume that made it hard to hear what was said in response to his stupid question. More sirens, undoubtedly summoned by urgent calls from terrified neighbours, were coming our way too.

Four cops, their faces a picture as they approached the two giant werewolves, kept their guns aimed as they got nearer.

'We won't resist,' said Garfield, meaning it.

A hand touched my shoulder, and I turned to find Alex. Now without the little girl she'd been holding. She looked down at me with a crooked expression. 'Damn, Anastasia, you look seriously hot in those new clothes.' She had to shout to make herself heard even standing right next to me.

I glanced down at myself. I was yet to see the effect in a mirror so was going to have to take her word for it. 'The My Little Pony hoody got trashed,' I explained. Suddenly self-conscious as Anton also came to admire my new look, I mumbled, 'The demons couldn't find clothes my size apart from this. At least, that's what they said. It's ... look just stop looking at me, okay?' I blushed. The stupid top made me feel like my boobs were sitting on a shelf and I wasn't sure about the exposed midriff at all. In my head, I looked like a slutty popstar about to start gyrating on stage for voyeuristic pleasure.

'Where's Daniel,' she asked, shouting still, but in the next breath the helicopter, which had already landed, took off again, powering into the sky as three figures came our way.

In the lead was a man with a military buzz cut which ended in a flat top hairstyle. I hadn't seen anyone wearing their hair like that in years. Under the streetlights, I could see it was silver grey and complimented the tanned and lined face to give the man the look of a hardened military commander. I had seen many in my time in the Army.

From next to me, Otto spat the word, 'Ironbolt.'

'Who is he?' I asked.

'Global head of the SIA and a man with one eye on being the US president. He would sell his children to climb another rung up the ladder.' Otto didn't like him, that much was abundantly clear, and it was good enough for me.

The cops had cuffed the SIA agents once Ayla and Otto rendered them unconscious, which Ironbolt saw as he continued forward. He passed between badly parked cop cars, side stepped the body of a fallen SIA agent and glared at our assembly of figures.

His eyes showed recognition when he spotted Otto which made his trajectory change slightly. 'Schneider!' he snapped. 'Report! What the hell happened here?'

Otto let his eyebrows rise to the top of his forehead. 'You know I don't work for you, right, Ironbolt?'

'That's President Ironbolt if you don't mind,' Ironbolt insisted.

Otto shook his head. 'You are not my president just as you are not my boss. Why don't you explain why you sent a squad to invade Ayla Pendragon's house?'

Ironbolt turned his eyes toward me. 'I see you have apprehended the fugitive Anastasia Aaronson. Well done,' he said, totally ignoring Otto's question the way a politician would.

'Fugitive?' I repeated, curling my lip at the word.

Ironbolt smiled at me, showing perfectly white, perfectly even teeth that would dazzle a crowd. 'Anastasia, you are wanted for acts of terrorism by several governments. I am here to see you are safely managed because I know you are one of the good guys.'

The cops had listened for long enough and tolerated the nonsense for as long as they could. This was their city and they were just going to arrest everyone and let the judge sort it out. They had only waited this long so that back up had a chance to arrive. There were bodies on the ground, and someone needed to answer questions.

It felt like the excitement was over.

Which made it the perfect time for the ice holding the demons to explode outwards in millions of pieces.

Chapter 36

The air filled with shards of ice which peppered everyone. I felt the sting as they caught my exposed flesh and heard glass shattering as larger pieces tore through car windows. The shockwave of the demons freeing themselves shunted me back – there wasn't enough of me to resist the outrushing energy. Staggering, I landed against Alex, whose greater body mass kept her in place, but now we had a new problem to deal with. The demons were free and though they needed a second to let the wounds from the ice spears heal, they would be killing again in a heartbeat.

It had taken Otto a lot of effort and more than twenty seconds to conjure the four icicles; it wasn't something he could instantly repeat. With only a split second to make a decision, and with so many targets around him, he snatched his shilt glove on and opened a portal.

'Everyone, grab hold!'

I heard his shout, but I was moving away from him, not getting closer. I was going to use my body to shield the mortals from the hellfire. If the demons wanted to throw it around, I would take all they had and give it back with interest.

Running at them now, I risked a swift glance over my right shoulder to see what Otto was doing. I did so just in time to see the portal snap shut with Ayla's family, DS Spencer, Anton, some of the cops standing closest, and even President Ironbolt, vanishing to the other side. Otto would bounce them in and out of the immortal realm, landing them back on Earth somewhere safe. I hadn't got the chance to get answers to any of my questions, but I had a new and far more pressing one to ask now.

'Alex, what the hell are you doing?'

The tall librarian was hot on my heels, running along behind me and keeping pace. 'I don't know!' she shouted. 'You started running!' she added as if that explained why she was charging headlong at four demons.

This was terrible. I couldn't hope to protect her with my tiny body. Ahead of me, all four demons were raising their hands, malignant grins stretched across their faces as they formed hellfire orbs.

'No, wait!' I yelled. 'If you kill her, we'll never find the other pieces of the armour!' They had been about to fire at me, though that was merely because I was right in front of them now. They might get me but I was a small target so they would get everything behind me as well. I made them pause though, just for long enough to add more words. 'Alex is a librarian.'

'That's right. I am,' she boasted as if it might scare them into behaving.

'She's the one who found the pieces in Osaka,' I assured them. 'She can find the rest.'

'I think I already have,' she chipped in gamely. I hadn't seen her in a day, since the early hours of this morning, and just like so many days recently, I was running on too little food and barely any sleep. Now I had stupid clothes to add to my list of woes. She had cracked the code to finding the artefacts though – unless this was a clever bluff – and though I wanted to keep her away from the demons, I could see no other way of stopping them from killing her where she stood.

Cop cars careened into the street, flashing lights and wailing sirens filling the air. Martha's head twitched to look and she loosed a pair of hellfire bolts that exploded the lead car.

'This is trivia,' I stated flatly, telling myself that only the way to stop them killing more was to make them leave. My eyes were on Aksel, the one I pegged as most levelheaded in the group. 'The armour is your mission, not a few annoying mortals.' I could see that he wanted to lay waste to all before him. The wizards had made them look less than the invincible force they believed themselves to be, and though they were able to shrug off the injuries, I knew they were smarting from the insult.

Mercifully, Aksel agreed with me. 'She is right. Take the big one,' he nodded his head at Bitrius.

'Hey!' complained Alex. 'That's a bit harsh.'

Bitrius snagged her arm, making sure he had flesh to flesh contact. 'Shut up, mortal, and prove yourself worth the effort or I'll shut you up forever.'

Alex almost spat a retort but closed her mouth before the words escaped and pulled her bottom lip over the top one to keep herself from speaking.

Martha was still blasting the cops with hellfire, laughing as they tried to reverse to safety while the lead car burned. The portal was open, but she looked set to stay and fight. Were it not for Acadus touching her so she was pulled through too, she might well have kept going until no one was left alive.

Leaving that hellish environment behind, where do you think the portal reopened?

Chapter 37

'**A**rrrghh!' screamed Alex as a sizzling orb of sinfire shot by her head. Wisely, she ducked, and I fired up my right hand as I put myself between her and the direction the light blue orb came from.

In all the excitement in New York, I had completely forgotten the glimpse of a fight we saw the last time we bounced through Beelzebub's house. Now we were right in the middle of it and survival for anyone less than immortal i.e. Alex, looked slim.

I yelled, 'Get down!' as I spotted a demon and sent a blast of sinfire her way. The she demon didn't see it coming as she looked for an angel to attack and it caught her in the head. Whatever happened to her escaped me because there were bodies flying in every direction.

'I am down!' yelled Alex in response. 'Someone give me a shovel so I can start digging.'

The generals waded into the fight without needing to think.

We were in a large room. It had a vaulted ceiling and many doors leading from it. Fighting was everywhere, but as the crowd parted for a second, I saw Beelzebub himself. He had an angel by his throat and as I watched, he raised the God sword to strike him down. The angel, not one I recognised, struggled and fought, but this was only going to end one way.

Unless I stopped him.

Beelzebub pulled his right arm back and I threw myself downward to get a clean shot. Sliding forward on my knees, I passed under the arms of an angel and demon fighting each other at point blank range and threw a sustained stream of sinfire at the ruler of hell.

It flew straight and true, right for his left ear. It wouldn't kill him, obviously, but it would throw him off balance and wreck his chance to kill.

Except it didn't.

Almost with casual aplomb, Beelzebub dropped the angel and used his left hand to deflect my shot. Then he swung the sword, taking the angel's head as he tried to scurry away. As the torso fell to the floor, Beelzebub looked my way and snorted a small laugh.

Someone shouted for the angels to retreat. I had no idea who might have led the charge to get into Beelzebub's private quarters, but it must have been because of the sword which meant Benjamin had told the angels about my capture. It reviled me that the angels were being killed, but I wouldn't allow myself to stop it because the Earth – humanity, at least – needed both sides eliminated if it was going to survive. Despite that, the angels were now trying to disengage, and the demons were trapping as many as they could.

If the angels could get into free space, they could conjure portals to escape, but with demons so close, that was impossible. I watched helplessly as Beelzebub skewered another of the angels. This time it was a female who screamed briefly before the source energy being pushed through her body ended her life.

I couldn't just watch, but I didn't know how I could leave Alex without guaranteeing her death. To accentuate my fear, a demon spotted me and started flinging hellfire my way. That I was doing my best to put myself between Alex and harm meant the hellfire was going her way too.

I wanted the sword back. Boy I wanted it, but with no way to wrestle it from Beelzebub's grasp, I had to make do with the gifts I had. The armour would have kept me safe from the hellfire anyway, but I welcomed it, this time enjoying the painful sensation as it tried to frazzle my senses. I didn't bother to spindle it, instead I channeled it straight back out, smashing the stupid demon across the room with a sustained blast. It lifted him from his feet and threw him bodily through another six of his kind like I was playing skittle with demons.

Alex whooped her joy, but we were far from safe yet.

In fact, in defending her, I made things worse, for the enraged demons, dozens of them now with no angels to fight because they were dead or had escaped, all turned their attention my way.

I screamed for Alex to, 'Hide!' and put everything into a stream of hellfire that I swept across the room like I was using a water cannon.

Her desperate voice shouted back, 'What do you mean hide! There's nothing here to hide behind!'

I couldn't risk glancing around to look, so I held the stream on and hoped for the best. Hellfire was still getting through, there were too many of the demons stepping up to put me down for me to get them all, but as each fizzing ball screamed toward me, I jinked left and right like a goalkeeper trying to make sure they hit me.

'Just keep your eyes open and make sure the red stuff doesn't touch you!' I shouted over the din of the fight. The hellfire striking me was just like the deal with Daniel in Osaka: recharging me while I used it. It hurt like hell, but wow did it work.

When an impossibly loud voice shouted, 'Stop!' everyone in the room bar me ceased firing. I knew who the shout came from just by the way the demons reacted and swung my eyes to see Beelzebub striding my way. I really wanted to slam him with my jet of hellfire, but I really didn't want to see him swat it away like he had my sinfire plus I needed to beg for Alex's life.

I dropped the stream, shutting it off and relaxing my pose. He still needed me, right? I sure hoped that was what he believed because if he thought otherwise, I only had seconds to live. Honestly, I held my breath until the moment I saw the light fading in the sword, but then I remembered he wouldn't need source energy powering it to kill me and felt my heart stop again.

The portal Aksel brought us through had opened at one end of the room and that gave me a great view from one end to the other. There was a small sea of demons looking at me.

'Can I get up now?' hissed Alex, still hiding behind my legs.

I shook my head no and continued to watch Beelzebub as he approached me. There was clear space between most of the demons and me because I had beaten them back, but he advanced beyond the nearest of them and into free space. Then he stopped, turned, and walked backward just a few paces to face the demons all looking his way.

He didn't speak straight away. He waited for the demons I had knocked down to get back up and dust themselves off first. 'Today was a test. An opportunity to see how it will be when the death curse fails. The angels came to us, invading our territory in a bid to retrieve this.' He thrust the sword high above his head. 'Many angels came. Fewer returned.' He got a cheer. 'They will come again because they have to and perhaps next time, they will be more organized. That my brother was not among them tells me this was not an attack which he sanctioned, and this is good.' His statement got a few curious looks. 'It means he no longer has full control. To come here without him, means they had to hide their intention from him. They are divided and we will crush them all the more easily because of it.' He got another cheer. 'It had always been the plan to go into the final battle against the angels after the death curse fell. We have waited so long to be able to defeat them, but it has been impossible because of the immortality we all suffer here. Not so anymore,' he added with a laugh in his voice.

He took a step to his side to better expose me and swung the sword at my center. He was going to skewer me, and I had no time to avoid the blow. I danced back but too slow to stop his thrust, the sword struck home.

Chapter 38

That the armour stopped it came as a complete surprise to me and to many of the demons too who looked disappointed the mortal woman survived. Beelzebub had known and tipped me a wink no one else saw when the sword's tip hit the breastplate and stopped.

He swiveled around to face his crowd again. 'Soon, I will have my father's armour to complement the sword and once I do, I will lead us to victory over the angels before the death curse fails. We will wipe them out or they can join us on the lowest rungs of our caste. The choice for those wise enough to surrender will be one or the other.' The crowd were baited. This wasn't his full demon horde, but it was a representative group who had received word of the fight at Beelzebub's house and answered the call to do battle. They would talk about this skirmish for centuries and those who were not there would feel angry or frustrated they missed out.

'Go now, my brothers and sisters. Go now and tell those who were not here of your victory. Tell them of the angels' audacity at striking so deep into the heart of our territory and how dearly it cost them.

Thousands of years we have waited to return to Earth, yearning for the days when once again our race will rule over the lesser species. That day will soon be here and now,' he punched the sword into the air again, 'our victory is assured!'

Roaring his final words drove the crowd watching him to a fever-pitch of excitement. They would be on a high for days. I didn't know how many angels might have attacked his house this day, or how many had lost their lives in the attempt to recover the sword, but they had been right to try. Beelzebub believed nothing could stop him now and I feared he might be right.

What could possibly be left to stop him taking over the planet? So far as I could see right now, once he added the armour, he would be invincible. As if hearing my thoughts, he closed the distance between us in one step and I could see his generals making their way back to my end of the room to join him.

Beelzebub's eyes were looking over my head to scrutinize Alex. 'She's with me!' I blurted. 'She's vital to finding the armour. Don't kill her.'

His eyes flicked down to meet mine. 'You are playing a dangerous game, Anastasia.' I expected more words to follow but his cryptic response was all I got.

I was left staring at him in terrified confusion as he walked away, and his generals arrived. 'You want your big friend to live?' asked Martha, her forehead creased as she glared down at me. 'You'd better do exactly as I say from now on or I'll hand pieces of her to you for a week.'

As threats go, it was a good one. It made my stomach lurch and I can only imagine the effect it had on Alex who got to her feet on shaking legs and held my offered hand tightly with both of hers.

Angry despite the victory they just helped to secure over the angels, Bitrius stuck the tip of his sword under Alex's chin, tipping her head back as the sharp edge bit into her skin.

I shoved myself between them, trying to physically shove him back. 'No! We need her!'

Leaning over me as if I weren't even there, he continued to threaten Alex's life. 'Where do we find the next piece of armour, mortal?' he demanded.

My efforts were rewarded by what felt like an elbow to the back of my skull from Acadus. It landed right where the skull joins the spine and made my vision swirl for a second.

Alex was going to get skewered if she didn't answer soon, but as I wondered if her claim to have the answers was a terrible bluff, she managed to sob, 'Saint Mark's Coptic orthodox cathedral in Alexandria.' I breathed a sigh of relief as I felt Bitrius let her go. 'There might be several pieces there.'

Grabbing my right arm tightly around the bicep, Martha growled, 'Let's get this done.'

Aksel was already opening a portal when I slipped my hand into Alex's. She glanced my way, her eyes full of tears and a line of blood coming from a small cut under her jaw where the blade had cut her skin.' For all the good it did, I gave her hand a squeeze. They were going to kill her the moment we had all the armour and I think she had already arrived at the same conclusion.

I was in deep trouble and I couldn't see a way to get out of it without help. Where the hell was Daniel?

Chapter 39

Daniel was still inside Beelzebub's house. He'd made it to the pit but found only a demon called Jerome there. He was trapped in a device that sandwiched him between two heavy plates set at a rough forty-five-degree angle. From the uppermost plate, dozens of long spikes skewered the demon in place through his body, his limbs and his head.

If the device had a name, Daniel didn't want to know what it was, and he never wanted to see it again. Suitably horrified, he confirmed Anastasia wasn't there and turned to go. Convinced she had to be here somewhere, he felt torn once more. He'd made it this far, but the longer he snuck about trying to find the girl, the more likely it was he would get caught.

A shout from behind as he made his way to the stairs made him duck his head and run. Had he been identified? Whoever shouted, it wasn't Beelzebub, but he was going to have to escape if he couldn't lose them. Ready to conjure a portal, he held off in the hope he might still find

Anastasia, but hitting the top of the stairs, he ran straight into a party of angels.

There was enough time for him and Benjamin to recognize each other before half a dozen angels hit him with sinfire. He tumbled backward down the stairs, the blast taking him from his feet so he was halfway down when his shoulder hit something.

There was no hope to return fire, but had he wanted to when he stopped tumbling, he didn't get a chance because the demons who had been chasing him arrived at the foot of the stairs. Looking the wrong way, Daniel saw Benjamin's eyes as the angel got to watch him be taken.

Daniel fought, but already weakened from the barrage of sinfire, the demons were able to easily knock him out with hellfire.

When he awoke, the pain hit him instantly and horror filled his veins as he realized Jerome was no longer inside the device.

He was.

Chapter 40

The portal opened into a darkened narrow street where I caught a strong whiff of sea air mixed with a familiar well-known fried chicken place. The smell made my stomach growl even as I looked around to spot the red and white restaurant behind me. It was warmer here. Much warmer. The kind of dry heat one gets in desert countries and welcome after the cold of New York.

Martha shoved my shoulder again. Smashing her face into the pavement in Mostar hadn't taught her a thing, or perhaps she felt more confident now that they had Alex and could threaten to kill her to keep me under their thumb.

I stumbled forward from the blow, stopping only when Alex, whose hand I still held, pulled me back. I didn't bother to glare at Martha, it wouldn't do me any good. Instead, I started walking, keeping hold of Alex's hand for her comfort more than mine and followed Bitrius and Aksel as they set off.

Around the corner, the cathedral was instantly in view, rising from the street to stretch into the dark night sky. Clouds above hid the stars like a blanket thrown across the sky. We were in the small hours now, I calculated in my head. The time difference between New York, where I had just been, and Egypt, where we found ourselves now had to be something like six hours. It wasn't something I had to work out before but we were not far from Zannaria now, where my left foot and left hand were still lying in the sand somewhere outside of a village with no name, and that was two hours ahead of the UK.

The time was irrelevant, of course. I had to retrieve the artefact, which when I drew in source energy, I could feel tugging me faintly forwards. Then we would move onto the next one, and the next one. I doubted the demons would let me rest no matter how many days it took to find them all, but with each new piece of armour collected, Alex's usefulness would dwindle until they had no further purpose for her. Before we reached that point, I needed to find a way to escape with her.

'You said this place might have several pieces here?' I prompted Alex, hoping that giving her something to occupy her brain might stop her from thinking about the demons.

She looked down at me. 'Yes, I think so. It was mentioned more than once. I found the same symbol you drew – the one from the wall in Rochester cathedral and then St Patrick's in New York, was repeated in journals and diaries of prominent religious figures. It was really patchy, of course, and we were doing it via the internet, not a proper research library, but more than one tied into Egypt suggesting the piece they had been entrusted with might have been moved here. There are many cathedrals across Egypt, I couldn't work out why this one was the one they chose, but it appears to be the case.'

'It is,' I murmured loud enough for her to hear. 'I can feel them.' My statement surprised her, but not so much as my question. 'Did you find any suggestion that there might be more weapons?'

Her mouth dropped open, but her eyes flitted about to see if the four demons had heard me. When they didn't react – we just weren't interesting to them – she swung her gaze back in my direction with eyes that begged me to keep quiet.

'How do you know about that?' she hissed.

I leaned in close. 'I don't know. The possibility has been suggested. Even Daniel said there might be more. I was very much hoping it might be true. It is?' I asked hopefully.

She shrugged. 'I have no way of knowing, but I found … I want to call them scriptures because that is what it felt like I was reading, but I guess notations is more accurate. Anyway, among the notations were drawings. Not many, I only found three instances and goodness knows how many thousands of pages I looked at, but one of them was for a dagger and if I am right, then it is here.' I let that information sink in and told myself to stay calm. She could be wrong. It could be gone, just like the shield in Mostar, or maybe there never was a dagger, or any other kind of weapon. Or maybe it was here but I wouldn't be able to wield it in the same way. The sword could kill the demons, but it didn't necessarily follow that source energy could be channeled through a dagger in the same way. There were too many unknowns for me to waste my time getting excited.

Despite that, I asked, 'How certain are you?'

Alex shot me a forlorn look. 'Heavens, Ana, I'm not certain at all. Listen, when you get inside, just run, okay? Don't worry about me. I'm just a boring, tall librarian with a slightly big bottom. They'll probably just let me go.'

I didn't say anything for a moment as we walked along side by side holding hands and sharing the lie that they wouldn't kill her if I ran away.

'You know I can't do that,' I said eventually.

She gave me a sad smile. 'What can you do? You told me they are immortal and the only weapon on the planet that can kill them is now in the hands of the devil himself. Once they have the amour there will be no further use for either of us, Anastasia.' She was no one's fool.

Nevertheless, I wasn't going to leave her to die. 'You'd better hope there is a weapon here then. I plan to kill them all.'

She gasped, but Acadus had heard me. He spun around to glare at me 'You want to kill me mortal?'

I laughed at him. 'Of course I want to kill you, stupid. What else could I possibly desire?'

Our conversation drew in the other three.

Aksel spoke next. 'How do you propose to do that? You no longer have the sword, little girl.' Boy, I love being called little girl. 'What is it that you think you can do?'

I smirked, quite deliberately, at him. 'Something surprising.'

Hellfire appeared in his right hand a second later, but he didn't waste his effort aiming it at me, his hand was pointing at Alex. I stepped in the way, but Martha raised both her hands with hellfire fizzing in each and a wicked smile on her face.

Our procession ground to a halt and it was one of those moments when the first to blink loses and I was sooo over being threatened. 'Go ahead bitches, kill her! Try convincing me to do anything if you do. Try finding the next piece of armour if I come back out of the cathedral and find her with so much as a split end in her hair!' I was already shouting, getting in all their faces and making them flinch as I lunged at their faces with mine. 'What do you think Beelzebub will say when you have no armour and no way of getting it? You just heard him. His entire plan revolves around having his father's suit of armour.' I saw doubt in Martha's eyes. It might have been reflected on the other demons too, but I wanted to kill her most and I was desperate to wipe the smile from her face. 'What are you going to do, Martha? Kill her. I dare you.'

Standing right on my shoulder Alex begged in a horrified sing song voice, 'What are you doing, Anastasia?'

Martha was fighting against her natural urges. She wanted to kill Alex and me both right now and was having trouble not doing so.

'She's doing the sensible thing,' I replied. I badly wanted to say that she was behaving like a good little doggy, and pat her face, but there was such a thing as pushing my luck too far.

To save me from myself, Aksel said, 'This is not the time, Martha.'

He tried to make his voice sound authoritative, but it did nothing to quell Martha's need to kill me. 'She insults me as if she were my equal,' she seethed. I bit my lip on the retort which found its way instantly to my lips, but I chose to hold her eyes, refusing to blink as she tried to stare me down. Then she reminded me, just how poorly matched we were. 'Just keep pushing me little girl. One more word and I will cut off your friend's hands. She won't die and will still be able to get us to the armour. If you say one more thing I don't like, make one more move I think suspicious, I'll carve off pieces of her until she is begging for this adventure to end and for me to let her die.

I gulped down my terror and regretted my need to stand up to bullies. It had rarely done me any good but now it was Alex who might suffer.

Acadus gripped my left arm, pulling me away from Martha's glare to shove me in the direction of the cathedral. 'Go. Fetch,' he pushed me away with a barked command.

When Alex's voice reached my ears, filled with hopeless acceptance, it almost broke my heart. 'Remember what I said,' she called after me.

All four of the demons narrowed their eyes at me, wondering what secret message she might be trying to impart. I just shook my head and told her, 'I'll be back in a few minutes.'

'Hurry,' suggested Martha. 'Lest I get bored and cut a piece off your friend anyway.'

I didn't think she would do it, but I couldn't be certain, and it terrified me that I might return with the piece of armour only to find Alex bleeding in the street. One might argue that it would make little difference when they killed her since it was clearly their plan. Die today, die tomorrow, what's the difference? Well, we all have to die some time, but I was going to put that task off for as long as possible. I included Alex in the same plan.

At the cathedral, I began to look around for a side entrance. I didn't want to blast the doors off the building if I didn't have to. However, seeing my hesitation, the demons united to all launch hellfire at the ancient oak entrance. Eight balls of hellfire were more than enough match for the ancient wood.

The doors didn't explode or rip from their mounts. They did, however, burst open, the last two orbs of hellfire flying through the gap to tear through the cathedral. I got to see them impact on the altar at the far end, turning the raised platform into kindling. I pulled in source energy once more, letting the tugging sensation draw me around to the right. Being able to home in on the other pieces made the task so much easier and I found the marker in seconds, dropping and reengaging the source to confirm the piece of armour was beneath my feet.

With a silent prayer to a God I knew did not exist, I looked down at the stone floor and told myself to think positive thoughts: there would be a weapon. There had to be, or Alex and I were never getting out of this.

Chapter 41

'You led this revolt?' Godfrey asked from his position reclined on cushions. His tent, which would more normally be filled with angels, had only a handful of loyal lieutenants in it now. Word of the attack on Beelzebub's house reached Godfrey's ears not long after it started when one panic-stricken angel bolted from the fight and arrived back at the angels' camp in a terrified state.

Now, all the surviving angels were back, and the finger of blame didn't take long to swing in Benjamin's direction.

'I did,' he replied defiantly.

'Leading how many of our brothers and sisters to their deaths?' Godfrey asked.

Benjamin narrowed his eyes. 'I do not know. Dozens I should think though it hardly matters.'

Godfrey snorted a laugh at Benjamin's statement, eyeing him skeptically. 'The death of our friends is of no consequence, you say?'

Benjamin was the only one in the tent from the attack. None of the faces looking at him were on his side and though he tried to keep emotion from his voice, he was angry, both at himself and at Godfrey for forcing him to act as he had. 'Beelzebub intends to kill us all and because of your refusal to act, he now has the weapon to do it. We had to strike before he reclaimed the armour as well.'

'Did you now? How did that go, Benjamin? I see you survived, which means you ran from the fight while others were slaughtered for your arrogance.' Godfrey's voice remained calm and quiet.

Benjamin's anger reached boiling point. He wanted to tear at the angels' leader, most especially for the accusation of cowardice. Through gritted teeth, he seethed, 'I called the retreat and got as many out as I could. Giannis had already fallen, as had many others, but it was a necessary maneuver and one we must repeat now before he has the armour.'

Godfrey made a show of chuckling at Benjamin's words. 'Go back? Indeed, I think perhaps you should, Benjamin. Let us know how that goes.' Then he rose from his seat and closed the distance to where Benjamin stood. 'There are many reasons my family has ruled this race, but the one which is key is our ability to strategise. There are many things you do not know, Benjamin. I have let my brother pursue the sword and the armour because it distracts him. I have accepted that he will cull the humans when the death curse fails because there is little I can do to stop it from happening if we wish to win. Your foolhardy attempt to snatch back that which I want my brother to have has done nothing but cost lives. I ask for loyalty, yet you have shown you cannot give it. We will beat the demons, and we will reclaim the Earth. Unfortunately, you will not be a part of the new world to come.'

Benjamin's head snapped across to look at the other angels seated around the tent. What was Godfrey saying?

'You are banished, Benjamin,' the angels' leader told him. 'Go now, and do not return. Your crimes would be punishable by death in any other society. Your lack of regret for your actions condemns you.'

Benjamin felt genuine shock. No one had ever been banished, but as Godfrey's words sunk in, he began to see through them. Benjamin posed a threat to Godfrey's rule. Angels might choose to side with him. He knew he was right about Beelzebub; the demons' ruler would lead assault after assault against them once he had the armour and would kill without concern until none were left. Godfrey seemed content to let it happen and that meant angels such as Benjamin must rise up to oppose his rule. Giannis had tried, gathering support as he demanded action, but he was dead now and with Benjamin banished, the opposition to Godfrey's rule would be more easily picked apart.

He saw no reason to delay his departure; Godfrey wasn't going to change his mind or allow anyone to change it. Plus, he could see from the faces of Godfrey's loyal supporters in the room, they were all in agreement and this was the senior council he was looking at, all bar a few members. However, just as he accepted his fate, Gabriel winked at him. It was a small movement that no one else in the room could see, but it meant something significant.

There were words he could say, threats he could make, but he held them all inside as he opened a portal and stepped backward through it. He had a vague plan, and it started with a demon.

Chapter 42

The stone slab beneath my feet cracked open, the piece I was standing on falling into the hole to spill me. Thankfully, unlike in Osaka, the hole was only about eighteen inches deep so I didn't fall very far. I did squeal in fright though as I tumbled in.

My blast of sinfire continued to dissipate outwards but the job of breaking through to the gap underneath was done with the first strike. Now I just had to heave the heavy pieces of stone out of the way which took far more effort.

Already grimy and covered in dead bugs and cobwebs, I discovered I wasn't strong enough to heave the wooden chest from the hole under the floor and had to resort to opening it where it was. Only as my fingers fumbled around for the catch did it occur to me just how large the chest was. The one in Osaka with the breastplate had been bigger, but not by much.

My pulse elevated as I opened it, praying I would find a magical self-arming cross bow inside, but as the lid swung upward, I could see it was just more armour. Two gauntlets, a pair of pieces designed to protect the upper thighs – I couldn't remember what the correct name for them was – the missing greave, and two pieces I had to mess about with to work out if they were for elbows or knees. I started to put the pieces on, each one vanishing the same as all the previous pieces to become an ethereal object floating just above my skin.

The helmet, assuming there was one, had to be out there still, but it now looked like I had well over half the suit and few pieces left to find. However, when I put the left-hand thigh piece on, I noticed a pouch built into it. Curious, I slipped my left hand in where it touched something just inside but out of sight.

When I pulled my prosthetic hand free, my heart stopped beating. I had seen one before on television but never dreamed I might get my hands on one. I didn't even know if it had a name but gripped firmly in my left hand was a throwing knife that came with a retractable lanyard to reel it back in like a builder's tape measure. The blade was two inches across, eight inches long, and black like the sword. The handle was like a knuckle duster that four fingers would slide into. The knife sat on the outside in line with my fingers so I could punch with it, though it was clearly made for throwing. In my excitement, I drew in source energy, planning to put the blade on my right hand to see what it would do.

The edge of the blade glowed, and I almost dropped it.

I held it with my left hand but somehow I had sent source energy to it. I tried again, this time lighting the blade from within and damned near freaking myself out with excitement. I pulled the knife from my hand to hold it in my right and looked down at my left. It was the gauntlet.

It had to be. Both hands were now clad in glowing blue light from the armour's gauntlets and suddenly I could conjure sinfire into either hand. That was amazing because I now had double the firepower, but far more exciting was a new weapon.

Exhaling slowly, I clambered from the hole and straightened myself. Would it work the same as the sword? I was going to have to find out. It was time to get back to Alex, that was for certain. I had stayed inside too long already, but I had to give myself a few more seconds just to see how the blade worked. Gripping it in my right hand, I folded my arm in to the left and flung it outward, picking a point directly down the aisle I stood in.

The blade shot off into the dark, continuing until it struck stone at the end of the cathedral more than fifty yards away. A flick of my wrist brought it snaking back to me, retracting along the line of the silvery metal, snake-like line which attached it. The blade part snapped back into the handle I still held. With my second attempt I discovered that it would return before it hit something if I so wanted which would be useful for when I threw it and inevitably missed my target. Then, because I spotted a statue, I threw it again, let the blade bite into the marble it was carved from and pushed source energy through my right arm.

The statue exploded.

I had wondered if the blade would work like the sword. My answer felt definitive.

A chill stole over me. I didn't know what would follow, but I was going to rescue Alex now and to do it, I was going to kill as many of the four as I could.

Chapter 43

Benjamin returned to the immortal realm moments after leaving Godfrey's tent. He didn't go to the angels' camp to rally support though, he could not be sure he would be welcomed there and were he to challenge his exile so openly, Godfrey would take other measures to ensure he could not return. He was without an ally, but one name instantly came to mind when he thought about gathering help to his side: Daniel.

The demon had been captured in Beelzebub's house. He'd seen it with his own eyes, and felt certain the outcast would be there still, held captive and unable to escape. Going back to Beelzebub's house was risky, some might even say stupidly foolhardy, but he saw few other options and the demons' lord would not expect a further invasion tonight. Furthermore, being alone allowed for stealthy movement and he could open a portal inside the house now that he had seen inside it.

Landing directly inside Beelzebub's house was fraught with the risk he would arrive in the middle of a room filled with demons, but it was a risk he committed to take. With source energy poised in his right hand for a swift exit, he opened a portal with his left and stepped through. He'd chosen a room he remembered close to where the bulk of the fighting had occurred. It was small and appeared to serve no purpose other than as a widened opening between corridors.

The portal closed behind him with a quiet pop, leaving the angel to hold his breath while he listened for any sounds. There were none to hear, the house was so silent he could hear his own heart beating.

This deep into enemy territory, Benjamin hoped to find Daniel swiftly, but sneaking soundlessly along the corridors, he only had to duck back out of the way twice as footsteps or chatter told him demons were coming his way.

By the time he found the outcast demon, Benjamin didn't know what part of the house he was in. It was only when, by chance, he came across the set of stairs he'd witnessed the demon fall down, that he found him at all. After edging down them, he discovered Daniel in a room designed for just one purpose: torture. There were no windows which made sense because descending the stairs had to have placed him below ground, but the room was harshly lit which showed off the single occupant.

Daniel was unable to form a portal to escape because both his hands were pinned with large spikes that went through them. The demon was to one side of the room where he was sandwiched between two metal plates. From the top plate, spikes protruded down into the bottom plate and out through the back where pools of Daniel's blood had gathered on the floor below. It horrified Benjamin to see any creature be treated like this. He betrayed Godfrey and was exiled.

Daniel was suffering torment that would only end when the death curse failed, and his body would stop trying to heal itself. Until then, the immortality element of the curse would keep him alive even if he wanted to die.

There was a mechanism on the side which Benjamin could see would unlatch to open the device, but it was closed and nothing he did would make it move. Benjamin went to the demon's side. 'How do I get you out?' he asked.

Daniel showed no sign that he had even heard him to start with, only the flicker of his eye a moment later, as it swiveled to look at the angel, indicated he knew someone was there.

'You cannot,' he croaked. 'It was locked by Beelzebub. Only he can open it.' Daniel sounded horribly wretched as one might imagine. His fate was sealed so far as he could see, and the fight was gone from him. He would suffer and then he would die. The only thing he could hope for was the death curse to fall soon so the suffering would end.

Benjamin bared his teeth in frustration, poking the device and looking at it from different angles. With his right hand on the handle, he pushed source energy into it and almost missed the barely whispered words the demon said next.

'Sustained stream. You need to form a sustained stream to open the device.'

Benjamin stood back, his eyes wide with hope. He knew of only three beings who could produce a sustained stream of source energy and only one who might help him. Getting his face as close to the demon's as possible, he begged him, 'Where is Anastasia? Are the generals with her?'

Unthinkingly, Daniel tried to nod and passed out from the pain. His immortality woke him a second later as the curse constantly tried to heal him. This time, he managed to look out of the corner of his eye. 'Cathedral in Egypt. More pieces of the armour. In Alexandria, that's all I know. I heard them talking about it.' Could he do it? Could the angel get him out? Then what? He decided it didn't matter what came afterwards because anything was better than this.

A cathedral somewhere in Alexandria was accurate enough; Benjamin was confident he would find them if they were still there. With a parting, 'I'll be back when I have her,' he opened a portal and stepped into the mortal realm.

Chapter 44

Emerging back through the broken doors into the wide street outside, I held my breath until I could see Alex still breathing. She was pinned in place by a hand locked around her left upper arm and she still looked ready to wet herself with fright. She was alive though and now I had a way to keep her like that.

The big question was when to deploy my weapon. Killing one of them might even be easy, but the other three would quickly turn on me, and with Alex close to hand, she would get killed in the first volley by accident if not directly as retribution.

The demons had maintained their respectful distance, unwilling to come closer to the religious building but they advanced a few paces now as I came toward them. Acadus, his grip on Alex's arm painfully tight, jerked her forward so she stumbled after him, but it was Martha who raised her right hand with a fizzing orb of hellfire in it. Alex tried to duck away, and the other demons looked at her in question as she held the hellfire close to the back of Alex's head.

'The suit of armour looks almost complete. I think we should call the job done, kill them both, and get back.' Her thoughts on the matter established, I could feel my left hand twitching toward the pouch on my left thigh.

'What about the helmet?' wailed Alex. 'There are more pieces yet.'

Bitrius stepped in between me and Martha, spoiling my shot, but also forcing her away from Alex. 'The mortal is right, Martha. The task is not yet complete. Cut a piece from her if you must but we need her alive for now.'

Rather than look disappointed, Martha reveled in his suggestion, dropping the hellfire in favour of a short sword she produced from a sheath on her back. 'Oooh, which piece doesn't she need?'

Alex screamed and tried to get away, but when Acadus changed his grip so he could hold her in place with both hands while Martha advanced, I knew I was out of time. I could wait for the right opportunity, but would Alex want to be saved by then? For all I knew, Martha was about to cut off one of her arms.

I was tipping my hand too early, and we were probably both about to die, but you can only play the cards you get dealt. Drawing in source energy, I powered myself up. The knife would naturally go into my left hand since it was on that side, but I felt more confident with my right so I reached across to pluck it from the pouch, largely ignored by the four demons who were enjoying their sport with Alex.

By the time Bitrius caught my movement from the corner of his eye, it was too late to stop me, and he caught my blast of sinfire right in his face. I wanted to whoop with joy that the shot had come from my left hand, but I was already lining up my throw and it needed all my concentration. I launched the blade, flinging my arm out and using it as an arrow to my target.

Acadus, Aksel, and Martha all saw it coming, but none of them could react fast enough to stop it. My aim was true, the sharp obsidian blade striking Martha right above her heart where it plunged through her clothing to penetrate her chest. Then I pushed source energy through the metal links that connected me to it and the glee I felt pulled my face into a terrible smile as Martha's limbs went limp.

Bitrius was getting back to his feet but all three male demons were too far away to do anything to stop me. If they threw hellfire at me, which I wished they would, I would just get stronger. However, my celebration proved premature for I failed to consider what else they might do.

Acadus tossed Alex to one side as he drew a sword from his belt. It swept upwards, slashing through the taut link between the handle and the blade.

The source energy powering it immediately shut off as the end still connected to the handle shot back to me. I stared in mute horror as Martha reached down to pull the knife from her chest. She looked at it, her face a mask of wonder which quickly turned to rage. The blade went to the ground, discarded roughly as she started running toward me. Her own sword came out as she closed the distance and she screamed, 'Kill the other one!'

With seconds to live, I drew in source energy and threw it all at her. I still held the handle for the knife in my hand, the finger loops ensuring it stayed in place, but my sinfire flew free despite it. The sustained stream hit her sword and deflected off, hitting a coffee shop across the street. The broad front windows exploded but I didn't see them. All I saw was Martha leap into the air with her sword raised high. She was going to bring it down right on top of me. More sinfire left my hands, but it passed through thin air as a blast hit her from the side, shunting her ten feet to the right.

Stunned by the turn of events, I looked around to find Benjamin running toward me. His next shot hit Acadus, bowling him over backward and suddenly, at least for a brief moment, it was two on two.

Showing good sense, Alex was running toward the cathedral, the one place she could go and be safe. Her arms were pumping, but whether she made it or not was down to me stopping the demons from launching hellfire in her direction.

Benjamin had caught them by surprise, but they were not stunned for long and knocking them down with sinfire again wasn't going to be easy. If I could get Alex to safety on religious ground, I could escape with Benjamin and come back for her later, but time moves fast in a fight and Martha was already getting up. The only thing working to my benefit was their reluctance to use hellfire on me. It meant they had to use elemental magic or get within physical striking distance of me which they couldn't easily do. Not with Benjamin on my side as well.

I ran to the angel, cutting off their option of hitting him with hellfire too and managed to throw myself into the path of the final two orbs they sent his way. Their power sizzled into me, overloading my synapses in a gloriously welcome way.

Then, side by side with an angel, we launched a sinfire attack. There was nothing Bitrius and Aksel could do as my sustained stream pummeled them, but Benjamin's efforts stopped with a gasp when an axe, thrown by Acadus, hit his chest. I couldn't hold off all four by myself, a flash of light from my left the only warning I got when Acadus threw a knife my way. I dropped to the ground, and in so doing had to shut off my sinfire.

Alex was almost at the church, but she wasn't going to make it. Martha had abandoned fighting me and Benjamin to stop the mortal woman reaching safety. A shot of hellfire hit the wall five feet in front of Alex, making her scream but also arresting her forward motion. Martha could kill her or toy with her, but she couldn't do that and fight me, so I pulled on my spindled hellfire and raised my hands.

And that was when I felt it. The handle still in my right hand was calling to the blade. It was still trying to retract the blade even though the link had been severed. I spun around on the ground to look for the blade forgetting Acadus and his throwing knifes. The next one hit me, the armour doing its job and protecting me from harm, but the impact drove me backward and knocked me off balance.

Separated from Benjamin, he was trying to remove the axe but now that neither of us were returning fire he was instantly pummeled by hellfire which Acadus rained down on him. Bitrius and Aksel were getting back to their feet and it was about to be four against one with Martha holding Alex hostage to force my surrender.

That couldn't happen, so when I focused again, I felt the handle call to the throwing blade and when I stretched out my right hand, it flew to me, a thin strand of source energy linking the two parts. The blade hit my hand, connecting with the handle again and I threw it.

Leaping back to my feet with a defiant roar, I watched the blade whip through the air. Magically reattached to the connecting snake of metal, it struck Acadus under his chin. His attack on Benjamin stopped instantly and he staggered back a step, his head barely connected to his body.

I ripped the blade out again, spinning to thrust my left hand at Bitrius and Aksel. They were just about to rejoin the fight, but a fresh stream of hellfire bought me the few more seconds I needed. The knife came back to my hand but only for a fraction of a second as I swept my right foot around and, like a discus thrower, I unfolded my arm at the apex and let it fly. I knew where it was going and this time Acadus wouldn't be able to stop me.

Even before it hit Martha, I was pushing source energy into it. I didn't have much hellfire left spindled inside me, but what little there was went out of me now.

I must have looked like a demented traffic cop, my arms out either side of me as I checked each way. The left was holding a constant beam of sinfire onto the three male demons. I had to keep changing my aim because I couldn't get all three at once, but the right arm was the one I needed to focus on.

When the knife hit Martha, I dropped my left hand and started walking toward her. The male demons would recover – I didn't know how long I had – but I planned to kill Martha and nothing else mattered.

Alex couldn't form a sentence. She was standing just a couple of yards from Martha, her eyes agog and her mouth hanging slackly open. She looked just as scared of me right now as of anything else. I would fix that later, after this was done.

The knife had hit Martha just beneath her solar plexus and to me it looked as if she ought to be able to pull it out again. However, just like a few moments ago when I first stuck her with it, her arms hung slackly at her sides and as I pushed yet more energy into it, she began to sag. Her knees buckled and though she fought it, she was at my eye height now and got to see my face up close as I came to a stop and gripped the end of the knife.

'You should be happy,' I snarled, rinsing every last drop of source energy from my body. 'I'm sending you back to hell!' My final shout echoed off the buildings as Martha's body fell back and away from me. The knife came free, snapping back onto its handle like a builder's tape measure winding in when released. The job was done though, the knife coming free because her body was crumbling.

'Ana!' yelled Alex, darting away in panic. Her shout made me jump, reacting fast by spinning around to see what had startled her.

It was the three male demons getting back to their feet. Benjamin too, had recovered enough from his beating to be stirring, but before I could advance on them, the three remaining demons fell backward through a portal I hadn't even seen them conjure.

The realization that I had killed one of the four horsemen of the apocalypse came with a sudden feeling of utter exhaustion. Yet again, I had gone days without sleep or food and my body was demanding I support its efforts by meeting its basic needs.

Benjamin was getting back to his feet when we reached him. 'You killed Martha,' he said. 'It was incredible.'

I lifted my right hand in which I still held the weapon and patted Alex's arm. 'Benjamin this is Alex. She is going to lead me to the rest of the armour. I need your help to move between locations, my previous guide appears to have abandoned me.' I didn't want to go after the armour. I wanted cheeseburgers and just enough beer to make me sleep twelve hours. I would have to attend to both things before we set off again but staying here wasn't an option. 'Take us to England, please. Anywhere will do but pick a city please because I need to eat.' Somehow, in all this, Alex still had her handbag with her which meant her credit and debit cards. We could eat and get a place to sleep.

That was until Benjamin spoke. 'Your previous guide? You mean Daniel? He is being tortured insane in the basement of Beelzebub's house. I can only free him with your help, Anastasia.'

'Beelzebub's house?' I repeated, confused. It dawned on my sleep deprived brain soon enough. 'He came after me!'

Benjamin nodded, opening a portal behind him. 'I believe he did, yes.'

Oh, wow. I thought the demon had come to his senses and ditched me for a safer option, but he'd risked everything to rescue me because he thought Beelzebub had me in his house. Beelzebub could have killed him. I glanced at Alex. 'I have to go,' I murmured quietly, wishing I didn't have to say the words.

A tear ran from her left eye. 'I can't go with you, Ana.'

'I wouldn't let you if you wanted to. We have to get you home where you will be safe.'

She shook her head. 'I'm staying here. It's a big city and I have money in the bank from savings plus credit cards. If the world is going to end, saving for a deposit on a house feels a little futile. Here.' She took out her phone. 'I'll buy a new one when the shops open and I'll call you. I'll carry on the research ...'

'I thought you found it all,' I questioned, interrupting her.

'I lied,' she smirked. 'I will find it though. I'll call and send messages. Don't worry about me, I'll find the British Embassy and work something out.' She was already backing away from me. 'This is where I get off.'

Though I knew Benjamin was waiting for me, I ran to Alex, sweeping her into a hug. She would be my partner in the mortal realm and most likely safer if I were nowhere near her.

After a few seconds, it was the wail of a police siren that made me break away from her. As I took Benjamin's hand and stepped through the portal, I got a look at her back as she hurried away and wondered if it was the last time I would ever see her.

Epilogue: Head of the SIA

President of the Supernatural Investigation Alliance, Colt Ironbolt was rattled by the last few hours. He would never admit that to anyone, but he had never expected to witness the things he did today.

When he started giving orders, the wizard, Otto Schneider, almost left him in the immortal realm as a demonstration of how little power Ironbolt actually possessed. It was only when he apologized to Ayla for the invasion of her home that Otto agreed to take him back to Earth.

That Ayla Pendragon was a powerful wizard came as a surprise. Ironbolt had read a report on her months ago when she returned from the immortal realm with Otto Schneider. It had caused a national news story because she had been missing for days after being taken from her house in the middle of the night. Her father, a man with the

President's ear, had made a lot of noise in drumming up investigative forces to solve the crime.

It also put Otto Schneider on the SIA radar, but the man refused to play ball. Tonight was his first encounter with the German, but now he understood why others said they could not control him. Perhaps Ayla would prove to be a better agent. He would recruit her and her policeman husband in the morning but sitting in his helicopter as the bodies of his fallen agents were dealt with back in New York, he wondered what good any of it might do.

He'd seen the demons and their power now. It was no longer a report in a file which he could read safely in his office. They were far more real to him than they had been before and their power seemed unmatchable, just as Otto Schneider described it.

The wizard said humanity could win, but a conventional fight would not work and that most of the weapons man possessed would be rendered useless by the magic the demons and angels could and would use. That was why he was trying to find the familiars he'd lost. In Otto's opinion, they were the strongest force on Earth when it came to fighting against the magical race because they had been using magic for hundreds of years in some cases. His determination to find them had placed him at odds with the SIA whose directive was to keep the supernatural phenomenon under wraps.

That had to change now. It was an epiphany for Ironbolt, who now perceived a new way forward for his organization. After the attacks across the globe two nights ago, the truth was out. They could try to put a lid on it again, but when he spoke with the president, a task that could wait until he was back in his office but no longer, he would advocate a new direction.

They couldn't go public and tell the people what was known about magic and demons; such a tactic would create mass hysteria and panic, but he could switch tack away from trying so hard to hide it and focus instead on finding and recruiting the supernaturals to form an army that could fight the demons when they came.

That's what he wanted to do, and he was in charge after all. Decision made, he closed his eyes and relaxed into his chair.

The End

Author's Notes

Hello, Dear Reader,

Thank you for reading my story. Since you made it this far, my guess is you feel the same way about Anastasia as I do – utterly in awe. Nothing stops her from doing that which needs to be done even though she openly admits she doesn't want to do it. Her path is a straight line from where she is to where she needs to be, constantly disregarding her own needs as secondary to the bigger picture.

I have put her through the wringer yet again and we are not done with her journey yet. With Benjamin at her side they will go after Daniel, not because she needs him, but because it is the right thing to do. My apologies for leaving you with that slight cliff hanger, but this is a story that must be told in chunks.

Anastasia, like Otto and Zachary, and characters yet to be developed, will all come together soon, for that is the only way the Earth and humanity can hope to defeat the ancient magical beings returning to the mortal realm when the curse breaks.

In this book I mention the war in the Balkans. I saw Mostar for myself in the early nineties when I was deployed there as part of the United Nations peacekeeping mission. The memory of how broken it looked stuck with me so that when I conceived the hidden armour – at some point last year – the idea that some of it might have been accidentally found through the ravages of war led me to choose that location. The shield is with another of our heroes, though I expect most of you already know that.

It is late summer here in the southeast corner of England where the temperatures are still delightfully warm. The colours are changing outside of my window though, the bright greens of June and July are fading away as the leaves begin to turn. Autumn is just a couple of weeks away now, and if you have been reading my ramblings for a while you know it is my favourite time of the year. Nestled in the rolling downlands with vineyards and orchards around me, plus castles, quaint villages, and more history than one can shake a stick at, the air here takes on an almost mystical quality each autumn. As the evenings draw in, the twilight hints at conker battles (kids whacking horse chestnuts for fun), chestnut stuffing for the Sunday roast, and woodland creatures preparing for hibernation.

We get hedgehogs under my log cabin each year which also means I get a dachshund under my log cabin as Mr Tank, the eldest and most accomplished hedgehog worrier, vanishes for hours sniffing around where they have made their beds. He cannot harm them; there's not much a dachshund can harm, but I have had to dig my way under to drag him out more than once.

I have a short break of maybe a couple of days now which I need to continue repurposing our rarely used dining room into a playroom for the kids. It feels like the right time to do it, and I am following my mantra of doing it right once. In this case, it means replumbing the radiator, fitting underfloor heating and rewiring lamps. Good thing I used to be an engineer.

I'd better get to it, actually, because I want to get back to the words – I have a murder mystery to write.

Take care

Steve Higgs

<u>**More Books By Steve Higgs**</u>

Blue Moon Investigations
Paranormal Nonsense
The Phantom of Barker Mill
Amanda Harper Paranormal Detective
The Klowns of Kent
Dead Pirates of Cawsand
In the Doodoo With Voodoo
The Witches of East Malling
Crop Circles, Cows and Crazy Aliens
Whispers in the Rigging
Bloodlust Blonde – a short story
Paws of the Yeti
Under a Blue Moon – A Paranormal
Detective Origin Story
Night Work
Lord Hale's Monster
The Herne Bay Howlers
Undead Incorporated
The Ghoul of Christmas Past
The Sandman
Jailhouse Golem
Shadow in the Mine
Ghost Writer

Felicity Philips Investigates
To Love and to Perish
Tying the Noose
Aisle Kill Him
A Dress to Die For
Wedding Ceremony Woes

Patricia Fisher Cruise Mysteries
The Missing Sapphire of Zangrabar
The Kidnapped Bride
The Director's Cut
The Couple in Cabin 2124
Doctor Death
Murder on the Dancefloor
Mission for the Maharaja
A Sleuth and her Dachshund in Athens
The Maltese Parrot
No Place Like Home

Patricia Fisher Mystery Adventures
What Sam Knew
Solstice Goat
Recipe for Murder
A Banshee and a Bookshop
Diamonds, Dinner Jackets, and Death
Frozen Vengeance
Mug Shot
The Godmother
Murder is an Artform
Wonderful Weddings and Deadly
Divorces
Dangerous Creatures

Patricia Fisher: Ship's Detective Series
The Ship's Detective
Fitness Can Kill
Death by Pirates
First Dig Two Graves

Albert Smith Culinary Capers
Pork Pie Pandemonium
Bakewell Tart Bludgeoning
Stilton Slaughter
Bedfordshire Clanger Calamity
Death of a Yorkshire Pudding
Cumberland Sausage Shocker
Arbroath Smokie Slaying
Dundee Cake Dispatch
Lancashire Hotpot Peril
Blackpool Rock Bloodshed
Kent Coast Oyster Obliteration
Eton Mess Massacre
Cornish Pasty Conspiracy

Realm of False Gods
Untethered magic
Unleashed Magic
Early Shift
Damaged but Powerful
Demon Bound
Familiar Territory
The Armour of God
Live and Die by Magic
Terrible Secrets

About the Author

At school, the author was mostly disinterested in every subject except creative writing, for which, at age ten, he won his first award. However, calling it his first award suggests that there have been more, which there have not. Accolades may come but, in the meantime, he is having a ball writing mystery stories and crime thrillers and claims to have more than a hundred books forming an unruly queue in his head as they clamour to get out. He lives in the south-east corner of England with a duo of lazy sausage dogs. Surrounded by rolling hills, brooding castles, and vineyards, he doubts he will ever leave, the beer is just too good.

If you are a social media fan, you should copy the link below into your browser to join my very active Facebook group. You'll find a host of friends waiting there, some of whom have been with me from the very start.

My Facebook group get first notification when I publish anything new, plus cover reveals and free short stories, but more than that, they all interact with each other, sharing inside jokes, and answering question.

f facebook.com/stevehiggsauthor

You can also keep updated with my books via my website:

g https://stevehiggsbooks.com/